ANIMAL RESCUE TEAM

Gator
on the
Loose!

ANIMAL RESCUE TEAM

1

Gator
on the
Loose!

SUE STAUFFACHER

illustrated by
PRISCILLA LAMONT

A YEARLING BOOK

All rights reserved. Published in the United States by Yearling, an imprint of Random House Children's Books, a division of Random House, Inc., New York. Originally published in hardcover in the United States by Alfred A. Knopf, an imprint of Random House Children's Books, a division of Random House, Inc., New York, in 2010.

Yearling and the jumping horse design are registered trademarks of Random House, Inc.

Visit us on the Web! www.randomhouse.com/kids

Educators and librarians, for a variety of teaching tools, visit us at www.randomhouse.com/teachers

The Library of Congress has cataloged the hardcover edition of this work as follows:
Stauffacher, Sue.
Gator on the loose! / by Sue Stauffacher ; illustrated by Priscilla Lamont. — 1st ed.
p.   cm. — (Animal Rescue Team)
Summary: Chaos ensues when Keisha's father brings an escaped alligator home to Carters' Urban Rescue, but it gets out of the bathroom while Grandma is guarding it.
ISBN 978-0-375-85847-5 (trade) — ISBN 978-0-375-95847-2 (lib. bdg.) —
ISBN 978-0-375-89539-5 (ebook)
[1. Alligators—Fiction. 2. Animal rescue—Fiction. 3. Family life—Fiction.
4. Racially mixed people—Fiction.] I. Lamont, Priscilla, ill. II. Title.
PZ7.S8055Gat 2010
[Fic]—dc22
2009018340

ISBN 978-0-375-85131-5 (pbk.)

Printed in the United States of America

10 9 8 7 6 5 4 3 2 1

First Yearling Edition 2011

Random House Children's Books supports the First Amendment and celebrates the right to read.

For my dear niece, Amara.
Welcome to the wonders of reading!

Chapter One

The call came in at 10:40 a.m. on Saturday of Memorial Day weekend. Keisha was at the desk, Razi and Daddy were out back bottle-feeding the raccoon cubs and Mama had taken the baby with her to the farmers' market. It was Grandma's turn to be at the desk, but she had traded with Keisha so she wouldn't miss her favorite show: *How Not to Look Old*.

Keisha looked at the ringing phone. It might be someone calling for information. But if her parents had to go out on a call, that meant Grandma would take them to the Grand River city pool's opening celebration. Grandma was not fun to be with at the pool. She made everyone wear big floppy hats, even in the shade. Plus, her swim cap had purple flowers on it, and instead of pinching her nose when she jumped in like everybody else, she wore a color-coordinated nose plug.

Keisha checked the caller ID and was surprised to see that it *was* the city pool. She picked up.

"You have reached Carters' Urban Rescue," she said in a deep voice. "Our office is now closed. If this is an emergency, please dial—"

"Is that you, Keisha?" It was Mr. Ramsey, the pool manager.

"Yes, sir," Keisha said.

"I need to talk to your mom or your dad."

"We're going to be there in an hour," Keisha said. "I'm working on my cannonball today."

" 'Fraid not, honey. You know that big alligator the kids climb all over? The one that spouts water out of its nose?"

"Mmmm-hmmm." When Keisha was little, she spent a lot of time climbing on that alligator and sliding down its tail. But she could go on the diving board now, so she didn't hang around in the kiddie area.

"Well, it appears it had a baby."

"A baby? As in a baby alligator?"

"That's affirmative."

Keisha got out an intake form. At least it sounded interesting. She wrote Mr. Ramsey's name at the top.

"Tell me what happened, Mr. Ramsey."

"This morning when I came to open up, there was a real alligator lying in the pool below the fiberglass one."

"How big is it?"

"Big enough to make me jump back over the fence. And I've got knee problems."

"That doesn't tell me how big, Mr. Ramsey," Keisha said in her calmest voice. "You have to talk in inches and feet."

Keisha knew a little something about alligators. She had written a report on them in Mr. Frost's class last year. Then she watched a special on TV. She loved the way they bobbed in the water with only their eyes showing. She planned to try floating like an alligator herself this summer. If Mr. Ramsey could give her an idea of the size, she could probably tell how old it was.

"Is it bigger than the spine board?" Keisha asked, referring to the board that hung on the wall by the locker rooms, the one they used if anyone had a bad accident at the pool.

"No . . . no, not that big," Mr. Ramsey said. "More like the rescue tube."

Keisha thought a minute. The rescue tube was

about three feet long. That was no baby lying in the city pool.

"Including the tail?"

"I would say the tail is extra."

"What about its snout?" Keisha asked. "Round or pointy?"

"Keisha. Do you really think I hung around long enough to take a look?"

"Maybe it's a crocodile," Keisha said, thinking out loud. "They have a reputation for being crankier, and—"

"Keisha! It probably doesn't *know* whether it's an alligator or a crocodile any more than I do. What I need to know is whether your mom or dad can catch it. I tried animal control, but everybody's got the holiday weekend off!"

"And the zoo isn't answering, either, I bet."

"Not the office phones."

Keisha nodded. The zoo had to cut their hours a few years ago. This meant that on weekends and holidays, Carters' Urban Rescue got a lot more calls.

"I'll tell my dad right now, Mr. Ramsey. He can be there in ten minutes."

"He can't get here soon enough for me," Mr. Ramsey said. "What am I supposed to tell my Little Minnows swim class? They were going to put on a synchronized swim show today."

"Better tell them not to get in the water."

"That's very helpful, Keisha. Thank you. I hadn't thought of that."

Keisha hung up the phone. When people were upset, they could also be sarcastic.

"Holy Missoni," Grandma said, making her way down the stairs. "My high-waisted jeans are strictly OL."

If you hung around Grandma long enough, you knew "OL" stood for "Old Lady." Grandma said your age was just a number and she chose number 48. Anything that was OL was not for Grandma.

"Grandma, there's an alligator in the city pool. Mr. Ramsey just called to tell us."

Grandma put her hands on her hips and looked past Keisha, thinking. Keisha could see that Grandma was trying to make the leap from jeans to alligators.

"Now, what would they want to do that for?" Grandma asked.

"They didn't do it, Grandma. It just happened."

"Do you mind explaining *how*?"

Keisha shrugged. "Will you answer the phones while I go out back to tell Daddy?"

"Maybe they're adding on some sort of petting zoo."

Grandma sat in the chair at the desk. "We got so many more visitors at the Twi-Lite Motel when the animals started coming around."

Grandma grew up in the Upper Peninsula. During the summers, she and Grandpa Wally Pops helped her parents run the motel. It was deep in the woods, and they had salt feeders for the deer, peanuts on the deck for the chipmunks—all sorts of animals visited and the kids loved it. That is, until black bears started coming to the hot dog roasts and raccoons figured out how to get the lids off the garbage.

As if Grandma was thinking what Keisha was thinking, she said, "I'm not so sure *that's* a good idea. We had a couple run-ins up there at the Twi-Lite that would scare the pants off of you—even tight, high-waisted OL ones."

As soon as Grandma was settled in, Keisha slipped out the back door.

She ran past the empty raptor cage and the squirrel enclosure before she got to the shed that housed the raccoon babies. Daddy was sterilizing the empty bottles, and Razi was using the special bottle rack that could feed six babies at one time, though at the moment they only had four. At this young age, baby raccoons were a lot like little kittens—so cuddly—but they didn't stay that way.

"Daddy, Mr. Ramsey just called. There's an alligator in the city pool."

Mr. Carter had strawberry blond hair and a fine sprinkle of freckles on his nose. He was tall enough to reach all the top shelves in the cupboard and skinny enough to stick his arm behind Keisha's dresser when her comic books fell back there. The best thing about him was that he always took you seriously. In fact, he said kids were smarter than adults sometimes. He would *not* ask Keisha if she was making this up.

"How big is it?"

"The rescue tube plus a tail. I bet it's a couple of years old."

"Maybe it came out of the sewer!" Razi said.

"That was just a story Zack and Zeke told us," Keisha said to Razi, who, at five, still had trouble telling the difference between what was real and what was make-believe. "Alligators can't live in Michigan. It's too cold."

"Maybe it came up here for summer vacation," Razi said as he finished feeding the sleepy baby raccoons. "Maybe it came up to visit relatives in the zoo and then it found out the zoo was closed for the day and then it got lost in that funny place downtown with all the one-way streets *and then*—" Razi paused to take in a big breath. Breathing was a problem if you were trying to tell an "and then" story.

But Keisha knew that once Razi got going, he could last a long time. Razi's record was sixty-two "and then's." By the time he said "the end" instead of "and then" when he told that story, Mama had finished her crossword puzzle and Grandma was asleep on the couch.

So Keisha rushed in with the words "I promised Mr. Ramsey we'd be there in ten minutes."

"We'd better get a move on, then."

"Can I bring my suit?" Razi asked as they walked back toward the house.

"Swimming's not likely with an alligator sighting, bucko." Daddy held open the screen door.

"They'll probably have to shock the pool with chlorine," Keisha said. "Just like they do after a baby poops."

"I don't want to wait until after," Razi said. "I want to ride on the alligator's back."

"I think you're confused about alligators." Daddy picked up Razi and set him on his shoulders. "An alligator isn't friendly like a dolphin or a porpoise. An alligator would be more likely to turn you into a snack than give you a ride on its back."

"Hey!" Razi said. "That rhymes! You're a poet and you didn't know it."

Keisha held the back door open, and Daddy bent down so that he and Razi could get through. When they got to the front desk, Daddy said to Grandma, "Looks like we have to go to the city pool to catch an alligator, Mom."

Grandma looked up from the computer screen. Keisha could see she was researching "jeans for the mature woman."

"What does 'stonewashed' really mean?" Grandma asked anyone who was listening. "That can't really be washing with stones, can it? Is that washing?"

"It doesn't sound clean." Daddy set Razi down and ran his fingers through his son's hair, thinking. "But back to the alligator . . . Maybe it was someone's pet."

"From what I know about alligators . . ." Grandma stood up and tugged at the waist of her OL jeans. "Well . . ." Grandma cleared her throat.

Everyone waited.

"An alligator's mouth is the exact size needed to fit its teeth, which are large . . . as far as teeth go." She opened the desk drawer, took out the truck keys and tossed them to Daddy. "Better get those raptor gloves."

"Good idea. We need to hustle. You coming?"

"Coming? Of course I'm coming. I like to be close to the action just as much as you do."

"I have an idea how we can do it, Daddy," Keisha said, tugging on her father's arm. "Catch the alligator, I mean. Do you still have that big noose . . . the one you used to catch the bull snake?"

"I do."

"Maybe we could bring that and some buckets for fresh water. I don't think chlorine is good for alligators."

"Just one minute while I get the beach umbrella," Grandma said as she stood up and looked around her. "Now, where did I put it?"

"It's in the basement with the inner tubes," Daddy said. "I'll get it. I want to get that canvas tarp we put under the tent, too. Maybe we can roll Ally up like a bug in a rug."

"You did it again!" Razi said. "You're a poet and—"

"—you didn't know it." Keisha finished for Razi and grabbed her brother's hand. "We'll wait in the truck."

Grandma took Razi's other hand. "Everyone's always in such a hurry around here. I suppose an alligator sighting means we're not going to work on our cannonballs today. At this rate, I'll be lucky to dip my toe in the water."

Chapter Two

Mr. Ramsey was out front to greet them. "It's still there," he said, as if, even now, he didn't believe it himself.

Grandma was reaching into her handbag for her extra-big bottle of SPF 50 sunblock. "Get on over here, girl," she told Keisha.

"As soon as we catch the alligator, you can put the lotion on." Keisha ducked out of the way and followed Razi, her dad and Mr. Ramsey into the pool office.

"Don't think you can escape me." Grandma waved the bottle over her head. "I'm going to be standing at the entrance. When you step out into the sun, you're mine."

"The rest of us can get a look at it from in here." Mr. Ramsey pointed to the plate glass window that looked out onto the pool. Keisha stared hard at the fiberglass alligator that stood at the very edge of the pool where the little kids played. It was so shallow you could walk right in after you got hit with the water that spouted from its snout.

There did seem to be something below it. Not a

very big something as far as a full-grown alligator was concerned.

"Here." Mr. Ramsey handed the binoculars to Daddy. "Have at it."

Daddy looked through the glasses. "Yup. That's your standard-issue reptile." He passed the glasses to Keisha. "Can't tell you for hundred percent positive sure it's an alligator until I get out there. Might be a big lizard. Maybe a Komodo dragon."

Keisha looked through the binoculars. It sure looked like something alive and scaly, but the legs of the big play alligator made it hard to see. Daddy started back to the truck to get his gear. Keisha didn't bother asking if she could go onto the pool deck with him. Daddy had told her many times that until she was an adult, he wouldn't allow her on any dangerous rescue missions. That meant eighteen, which also happened to be the age to get a tattoo—if she wanted one of those—or to pierce anything besides her earlobes.

"Can I at least go look at it from outside the pool fence?" she called after him.

"Me too! Me too!" Razi was hopping on one foot. The other was curled around his knee.

Daddy turned around. "Bathroom first," he and Keisha said at the same time.

As Keisha took Razi's hand and began pulling him toward the locker rooms, she called back to her dad, "If you wait a minute, I have a couple of ideas."

"Let me get suited up first."

Keisha headed toward the women's locker room but Razi pulled back. "Mommy said when I was five, I could do it myself."

"Razi, *please* . . ." Keisha just wanted to get back to the action. But as hard as she pulled, Razi resisted. He was getting strong! "Fine, but don't take forever . . . and wash your hands."

Razi disappeared through the doorway of the men's locker room. After a minute, Keisha called through the tiled entryway, "No breathing on the mirror and writing your name. No unrolling the toilet paper."

After three minutes, she knew something had caught her brother's attention. "What are you doing in there? I'm counting to ten and then I'm coming in. . . ."

Keisha counted to herself so she could skip a few numbers. As soon as she took one step inside, she bumped into Justin, the head lifeguard. He didn't see Keisha because he was patting his face with a towel.

"Hey, Keisha. I was shaving. Mr. Ramsey doesn't like it when we look scruffy. You can go on in. There's nobody in there but Razi, and he's looking into one of the toilet bowls."

Keisha curled up her toes with their pretty painted nails to keep her flip-flops tight. She had never been in the men's locker room before. But she had to get her brother. He was on his hands and knees in one of the bathroom stalls, looking into the toilet bowl. Just as Keisha reached him, he leaned forward and flushed, watching the flow of the water with great concentration.

Keisha grabbed his arm. "Come on, Razi. We've got an alligator to catch."

"I was just thinking," Razi said, "about how he got here. Wouldn't he get drownded if he was flushed down the toilet and then swishy-swashed through all the pipes and then emptied into the pool?"

Keisha sighed. You never knew where Razi's imagination would take him. She had to be careful not to rush her brother. If she did, he would lock his arms around the toilet bowl and hold on for dear life. From experience, Keisha knew that when she tried to get Razi to do what *she* wanted him to do, he almost always fought back. It went faster when Razi thought it was his idea.

"Razi, if you let me show you the real alligator outside, I can explain it. You see, alligators are pretty much waterproof. They have little flaps that close over their nose and their ears, and they have more than one eyelid—it's like wearing a pair of swimming goggles all the time."

"Do you have to pay extra for those or do they come with the standard model?" Razi was now staring up at the cement-block wall. He had the same look of concentration he got when Daddy took him down to Bishara's Friendly New and Used Auto Emporium.

"It used to be extra, but it's standard-issue on all new models," Keisha said, circling her fingers around Razi's wrist. "What's even better . . ." She waited until Razi got to his feet and started to follow her. He had that faraway look in his eyes, like he was imagining what it would be like to have swimming goggles on all the time.

"What's even better is that they can close off their throats, too, and be airtight. An alligator can stay underwater for twenty minutes, no problem, but"—Keisha made one more dramatic pause to get Razi out into the sunshine—"if it's colder and its body slows down, an alligator can stay underwater for up to eight hours, Razi."

"I want to see the standard-issue swimming goggles!" Razi broke free of Keisha and rushed for the fence that enclosed the pool. Grabbing on to it with both fists, he set up a playground-sized clatter. It was enough to scare the fiberglass alligator, let alone the little one underneath. Keisha thought she saw something move. Was that the alligator? Even outside the fence that surrounded the pool area, they were still too far away to see well.

Grandma was scanning the water from the other side of the pool. She stood on the pool deck near the entrance by the lifeguard station. That was the only way to get into the pool—besides coming from Mr. Ramsey's office—so the lifeguard could see if you hadn't showered or could blow his whistle if you were so excited to get into the nice cool water that you ran on the deck.

Nice cool water, nice cool water. Ooh! That gave Keisha an idea. She waved her arms at Daddy as he emerged from the pool office in his big waders and the heavy

canvas gloves he used for the raptors. He was dragging the canvas tarp with one hand and holding the fishing rod with the noose attached to the end with the other.

Daddy always swaggered a little when he put his waders or his big gloves on.

"Daddy," Keisha said when he got close enough. "What does the pool water feel like?"

Daddy removed a glove and leaned over. "Cool," he said. "Ahhh . . . cool. You think the little guy is going to stay put?"

"Who is going to stay put? Why?" Razi wanted to know. He was tugging on Keisha's arm. "When can I see the goggles?"

"Alligators are poikilothermic, Razi," Daddy told him. "That means cold-blooded. You are warm-blooded and can stay warm even when it's cold by putting on sweaters and mittens. Cold-blooded animals like alligators and snakes get as cold as it is outside their bodies, and then they just—"

"They freeze up," Keisha interrupted. Razi didn't care about the science as much as she did. "Daddy, if you go slow, maybe you can put the noose around his snout. If his mouth is closed and we can catch him, then we can roll him in the tarp."

"That sounds like a plan. As I recall, alligators have

lots of muscles for clamping down, but not opening up. Their mouths are easy to hold shut."

"If he's frozen, how come he's running away from Grandma?" Razi asked, turning everyone's attention back to the pool.

Later, Keisha would think that the sight of her grandma rushing toward that poor little alligator and waving her arms like she did when she was rooting for the Langston Hughes Elementary School girls' basketball team—from an alligator's-eye view—would have been enough to make his blood run cold even if the pool water had warmed up.

Grandma was shouting, "Get ready, Fred. I'm sending him your way!"

It seemed like a good idea, but it didn't quite work the way Grandma thought it would. Instead of running away from Grandma and across the pool deck, the alligator scuttled deeper into the water. After a few kicks, he was able to dive down and swim underwater all the way to the deep end.

Daddy looked back over at Keisha.

"FTC," they said at the very same time.

"FTC" stood for "Failure to Communicate." When you worked with scared or injured wildlife, you needed to stay calm and have a good plan. Failure to communicate was one of the Carter family's biggest problems, *especially* when Grandma was in on the rescue operation.

Mr. Ramsey had rushed out to Grandma. He helped her back to the pool office by holding on to her arm— very OL—and was looking over his shoulder as if some monster had just jumped into the pool and not a poor scared alligator that was barely the size of the rescue tube.

"Looks like it will be Plan B," Daddy said as he leaned back against the fence and crossed his arms, which made his waders squeak impressively. "Remind me again about Plan B?"

"The problem with catching him is that alligators can see all the way around their head . . . and they can feel when anything enters or leaves the water."

Daddy crossed his arms the other way. "Goodness, this sounds like something the United States Army would be interested in."

"Hmmm." What Keisha wanted was to jump over the fence and get into the action herself. She was small enough to lie on the diving board and not let a shadow fall onto the pool. But she took one look at Daddy all covered up and decided not to even ask.

"They don't have big lungs, so they can't move fast for long. You could chase him around the pool until he gets ti—"

Keisha stopped. "What was that?" An alligator's eyes were peering at her from the deep end of the pool. He was swishing his tail back and forth in the water!

She took Razi's hand and pointed.

"He's trying to get warm," Keisha told Razi. She looked at the dark tarp absorbing sun on the pool deck, where Daddy had let it fall in a pile.

"I think he knows he has to get out of the water, Daddy. If you go throw the tarp over that play alligator, he might want to hide underneath it."

Grandma was back on the pool deck waving the pole with the net attached, the one they used to skim off the leaves and bugs from the surface of the water.

That gave Keisha another idea. "Maybe we should get a bigger alligator to scare the little one!"

Daddy looked at Keisha over his shoulder. "Say *what*? Don't you think one alligator in the city pool is enough?"

"It doesn't have to be a real alligator. The little one just has to think so."

It took Daddy a minute to warm up to Keisha's idea, but then it must have clicked because he cupped his hands around his mouth and yelled in the direction of Grandma: "Mom! CFC."

"CFC" stood for "Carter Family Conference." Most times when the Carters had a Failure to Communicate, they needed to follow it up with a Carter Family Conference.

Daddy grabbed the tarp and took it over by the fiberglass alligator. He tossed the tarp over it and tucked all the loose ends under. Keisha wondered if such a place would look warm and safe—like a hole on the riverbank—to a little alligator.

Grandma let her net drop to her side and put her hand on her hip. Keeping close to the fence, Daddy walked around and whispered a few things into her ear. Grandma whispered back and disappeared into Mr. Ramsey's office.

The next thing Keisha knew, Justin was taking the spine board off the wall and he and Mr. Ramsey were carrying it through the pool office.

Razi tugged on Keisha's arm. In all the excitement, she'd forgotten about her little brother.

"What are they doing now, Key?"

"I'm not sure. Let's watch."

Razi grabbed hold of the fence and started reciting one of their hand-clapping rhymes: "In came the doctor, in came the nurse, in came the lady with the alligator purse."

"Razi, not so loud. We want the alligator to come back by us. Shhh . . . look."

Justin and Mr. Ramsey trotted past them, just inside

the fence, with the spine board. Mr. Ramsey couldn't stop looking over his shoulder for the alligator.

"Where are you going?" Razi asked, and took off after them. "Can I come? Can I ride on that?"

The fence by the deep end was only about fifteen feet from the pool. Justin and Mr. Ramsey stopped there. It looked like they were waiting for Daddy's signal. Keisha watched as Daddy walked slowly back to the fiberglass alligator in the shallow end. As soon as he took his place, he waved at Justin and Mr. Ramsey. They began heaving and ho-ing, and that's when Keisha knew what had been decided at the CFC. On the count of three, the spine board sailed through the air. Nothing makes a small alligator get out of the water faster than what he thinks is a big one, because it is a little-known fact that alligators eat each other! If you didn't know any better and you were a small, scared alligator, you might think the spine board was a very big alligator.

When it landed on the pool surface, that little alligator dove down so fast it was hard to keep track of him.

"Where is the little bugger?" Grandma had put on her sun visor and was scanning the surface of the pool.

Keisha had better eyes. She saw him scuttle out of the water and dive under the folds of the canvas tarp.

Daddy did, too. Quick as a flash, he was there, stepping on the open end with his big waders.

Mr. Ramsey called out, "Need any help over there?"

Grandma was power-walking over to where Daddy was busy making sure there were no avenues for escape.

"I think we've got it covered," she said.

"There *is* something you can do," Daddy called back to Mr. Ramsey. "Will you get the dog crate from the back of the truck and maybe a hamburger patty from the snack bar?"

"Sure, but it's frozen."

"Never mind, then. This little guy is cold enough as it is."

Grandma stood over the tarp with her hands on her hips. "I was hoping this wouldn't take all day. I don't know about you-all, but I've got work to do."

"On Saturday?"

"I'm designing my own jeans. Mid-rise, boot cut . . . generous, kind to the silhouette. I'm thinking YSL."

"Yves Saint Laurent?" Keisha had been around Grandma long enough to know some of the fashion designers she liked.

"No, no. Mid-rise, boot cut . . . it all adds up to Youthful Senior Legs."

Chapter Three

Mrs. Carter grew up on a ranch in Nigeria. Nigeria is on the western coast of Africa right near the equator. Half the year, it is dusty and hot. Half the year, it is rainy and hot. In Nigeria, there are tropical rain forests and deserts and almost everything in between. Mama grew up near the Jos Plateau, in a vast grassy area called a savanna.

During the dusty times, Mama often had to sweep twice a day. She had always liked things tidy, even now in Michigan, where half the year the dust was frozen! Mama also liked to keep the animals out of the house. She knew that there were times when you had to bring the animals in, such as when they were babies or very sick. But she reminded her children many, many times that the goats and sheep they raised in Nigeria were kept in pens on the other side of the courtyard from the house.

For all these reasons—lots of animals, enough dirt already—Mama was not interested in any CFPs. "CFP" stood for "Carter family pet." The only person in the Carter family who used this abbreviation was Keisha. It used to be when she went to her friends' houses and saw their puppies(!), their kittens(!), their gerbils(!) she would ask Mama if she would think about changing her no-pets rule. But Mama knew what Mama knew, and Keisha's mama did not want one more animal in the house.

That was why when Mama carried baby Paulo into the house, all the other Carters sat quietly in the kitchen, picking at their peanut butter and banana sandwiches. No one knew how to tell Mama about the alligator upstairs in the bathtub, with Grandma outside the bathroom door reading her *Harper's Bazaar* magazine for denim inspiration.

Grandma wasn't guarding the door because the Carters thought the alligator would open it. She was guarding the door because, as with everything
else in the very old
house, it was hard to
make it stay shut on its
own. In all the excite-
ment of bringing home
their first alligator, no

one could find the big skeleton key that locked that door.

"One sticky baby," Mama said, giving Daddy first a kiss and then the baby. Paulo liked to dangle. Daddy just let him hang there in the air, a smile on his adorable face. He was chewing on a Popsicle stick, and Popsicle juice was all over his hands and down the front of his jumpsuit.

"Where's Grandma Alice?" Mama asked, setting down a string bag full of vegetables from the farmers' market. "Keisha, when you are finished with your sandwich, I want you to go up and run the bathwater so Daddy can give the baby a bath."

Keisha and Daddy and Razi looked at each other and then back down at their plates.

"Look at these greens," Mama said, holding up a bunch of spinach so the children could admire it. "After I rinse them, they're going in the pepper soup."

Most people didn't make soup in the summer, but Mama had a pot bubbling all year long. She especially liked to make red pepper soup out of tomatoes and peppers and chicken broth. Then she added whatever meat and vegetables she had around.

In Nigeria, guests expect to be fed when they stop by, and it is considered rude if you don't have enough food to offer them. Mama made food for her family as well as food for anyone who liked to drop in. The postman, Mr. Sanders, loved Mama's pepper soup. He said it was the only thing that cleared his sinuses. Mama's soups were spicy. That was how she'd learned to make them. A lot of Keisha's friends said "No thank you" when Mama offered them soup.

"Razi, what are you doing with your lips?" Mama asked in her and-don't-pretend-you-don't-know-what-I'm-talking-about voice. Razi was pinching his lips together. Keisha knew exactly what Razi was doing. He was trying to keep the secret in.

"Don't forget to breathe, son," Daddy whispered.

Razi took in a big, noisy breath through his nose.

"There's something wrong here," Mama said, her hands on her hips. "What is caught inside your mouth, Razi? Tell me now."

"But, Mama, you're the one who says the mouth should not relate everything the eye sees," Keisha reminded her mother.

"Yes, but that does not include keeping secrets from Mama."

"Well . . ." Keisha looked at her dad. There wasn't much hope of keeping it hidden.

"There's an alligator in the bathtub," Razi blurted

out, panting hard. He had forgotten to breathe. "Want to see it?"

"There's an alligator in *my* bathtub?" Mama repeated, taking baby Paulo back and cradling him in her arms. She must have been in shock because Paulo put his sticky fingers all over her necklace and she didn't even notice.

"It's Lyle, Lyle, Crocodile, only it's an alligator and it doesn't talk, but it has goggly eyes that can see behind its head!"

Keisha sighed. When Razi tried to keep a secret, it was like putting a kink in the hose. Once you undid the kink, the water spurted everywhere.

"Now we need Hector P. Valenti to come and take him back to the circus," said Razi. "When I grow up, I want a mustache like Hector P. Valenti!"

"Hector P. Valenti?" Mama turned to Keisha and raised one of her eyebrows, just a bit, which usually meant *Child, you are getting on my last nerve!*

"We heard a story about a crocodile named Lyle at story time yesterday," Keisha said. "In the story, he lived with a family, but his real owner worked in the circus."

"His mustache was this long." Razi flung out his arms. "And stiff. Daddy said you could hang an umbrella on it."

Now it was Daddy's turn to get Mama's high-eyebrow look. Everyone knew where Razi got his talent for exaggerating. "Not a beach umbrella," Daddy said. "More like a parasol. Anyway, Mr. Valenti's mustache is not the point here. We're not set up for large reptiles out back, Fay, and we had to get the chlorine off him."

Mama pulled out a kitchen chair and sat down. The baby was in her lap, and the greens were in his. Paulo squished the spinach with his little fingers and smiled.

"You were going to the city pool," Mama said, trying to piece it together.

"That's where we got him!" Razi told his mom. "Grandma yelled him into the deep end and then the spy board scared him into a big bag."

"Spine board, Razi." Keisha turned to Mama. "It needs to get a little warmer before he can be outside. We could make a little shelter. Just until we can figure out what to do with him."

"I wanted to run through the sprinkler with him, but Daddy said that would make some chaos," Razi informed his mother.

"I said 'cause chaos,' buddy. Can you imagine what the neighbors would think of us if we put the alligator in a purple polka-dot bikini and let it run through the sprinkler out back?"

Whenever Mama looked like she was going to get mad, Daddy tried to jolly her out of it by saying something funny. The fact that Mama was not smiling now was a sign that an alligator in her bathtub made her very unhappy. She stood up again, holding Paulo close on her hip. She went to the stove and turned the gas on low under her soup. Setting a bowl in the sink, Mama pulled the bunch of greens from the baby's hands and dropped them in. She let Paulo dangle over the sink and swish his hands in the water to rinse off the sand and grit.

"Can this really be the same bathtub, Fred, that just got the new enamel? What will alligator toenails do to my new enamel?"

"We put a wet beach towel underneath him. I'm hoping that will protect it."

Mama handed the baby to Keisha and tossed the rinsed spinach into the pot. Then she picked up the bowl of rinse water, carried it to the back door and poured the water over the roses that grew by the step.

"So tell me," Mama said when she had dried out the bowl and put it back in the cupboard. "How big is this alligator that is not in my tub?"

"Not too big," Keisha told her mom. "Maybe three loaves of bread and a tail?"

"And does that make it a baby?"

"Well, not exactly. But he was crying for his mother."

Mama looked over her shoulder at Keisha. She never could stand to hear a baby cry. "How do you know that?"

"I'm not positively sure," Keisha said, unsticking a banana from some peanut butter and popping it into Paulo's mouth. "But in my report, I learned a little something about how alligators communicate, and that's what I *think* he was doing. But it's a lot different reading about it in a book and hearing it in real—"

"It crawled out of the bathtub!" Grandma yelled down from the top of the stairs. "Want me to get some towels?"

Daddy tilted back in his chair and turned to face the doorway. "Just make sure to keep the door closed, Mom."

Keisha knew from the look on her mother's face that Mama understood now there really, *really* was an alligator in the bathtub and this wasn't just one of Razi's make-believe stories or Daddy trying to pull her leg.

"Sorry?" Grandma yelled back. "I'm getting some feedback in my transmitter."

Though she hated how OL they looked, Grandma

did have to wear hearing aids. It helped some that they came in designer colors now and not just "flesh."

"The door, Mom. Make sure the bathroom door stays closed."

"Why should I answer the door when you-all are so much closer to it?"

Everyone froze, listening to the sound of Grandma clattering back down the hall.

"Jumpin' Jimmy Choo," she said. "Where'd it go now? I could swear that door was closed."

Chapter Four

The entire Carter family, except baby Paulo, knew right away what had happened. They knew right away because this was not the first time that Grandma had lost an animal. In fact, over the years since Daddy had brought his mom to live with them at Carters' Urban Rescue, she'd also lost a sugar glider, a pregnant possum and a rat snake.

Daddy dashed upstairs. Mama took the baby out of Keisha's lap and set him in his high chair. "Keisha, you keep the baby in here. And *do not* let Razi out of this room."

"But, Mama, I—"

"Do not 'But, Mama' me now, Ada. That alligator could bite off your toe!" And she rushed out after Daddy.

In Nigeria, "Ada" was the word for "first daughter," and Mama always called Keisha that when she wanted her to act like a grown-up. It would help if Keisha's family could learn to stay calm during an emergency. If Mama had thought it through, she would realize how unlikely it was for a small, scared alligator to bite off anyone's toe. Alligators did not nibble at their prey the way you would an olive on the snack table. They dragged it under the water, drowned it, let it get all mushy and soft and then shook it hard until it broke up into bite-sized pieces. To get your toe bit off, you'd have to practically set it right into the alligator's jaw.

Keisha glanced over at Razi.

Well, in his case, Mama might have a point.

"Ding-dong," Mr. Sanders, the postman, said as he knocked on the back door. "Mail's here. Mmmmmm. What is that delicious smell?" Mr. Sanders always said "ding-dong" even though he knocked on the back door, and he always said "What is that delicious smell?" because there was always something delicious cooking in Mama's kitchen.

"Soup! Did I get my package?" Razi loved to see Mr. Sanders. He was certain he was going to get a package, though he didn't know from whom. But the package never came.

"I'm sorry to say there is no package for Mr. Razi Carter. However"—Mr. Sanders rummaged through his bag—"when I opened my cereal box this morning, I found this little item, and it had your name all over it."

"Where?" Razi asked, looking at the crinkly plastic packet that Mr. Sanders held out to him.

"It's just a saying," Keisha told Razi. She took the packet from Mr. Sanders and put it on the counter. "First things first, Razi. Say hello to Mr. Sanders."

"Hello to Mr. Sanders," Razi said, stretching his arm over the counter to reach where Keisha had placed the packet. "I want to see my name, Keisha."

"Your name isn't on it," she told her brother. "It's a way of saying that Mr. Sanders found something you would like."

Why did Keisha have the feeling that the gift wasn't something *she* would like? The cereal-box toy looked as if it made noise. While Razi was fond of things that made noise, the rest of the Carters were not.

"What is that long face for?" Mr. Sanders asked Keisha. "I don't suppose this would cheer you up. It's for our soup." Mr. Sanders pulled a fat white vegetable from his pocket and held it out for Keisha to see.

"A potato?" Razi guessed.

"Good guess, but no."

"Hmmmm . . ." Keisha took the vegetable in her hand. Last year, when she was having trouble remembering her countries for geography, Mr. Sanders would quiz her by bringing vegetables from around the world. Usually the vegetables ended up in Mama's soup, but first Keisha would check her big map to see the country

they came from. It was much easier to remember something you held in your hand and could taste and feel than names printed on a sheet of paper.

"I'll give you a hint. Its nickname is yam bean."

"Then it must be from Nigeria," Keisha said, "because they love yams in Nigeria."

"Nope. I didn't want to tell you its full nickname because that would give it away. But another nickname would take you to a whole different continent."

Keisha gave the yam bean back to Mr. Sanders. She wasn't in the mood for a vegetable mystery. Normally, she would like it, but right now what she needed to do was figure out how to find an alligator. She took two small steps backward to be closer to the door to the hall.

"It's called either a Mexican yam bean or a Chinese turnip. Go figure. But its real name is jicama, and it is a staple in Central America."

"Hee-ka-ma, hee-ka-ma!" The way Mr. Sanders pronounced the word sent Razi into a bounce. Bouncing also got him closer to the packet on the counter. "Do alligators like hee-ka-ma?"

Mr. Sanders didn't seem at all surprised by the way Razi changed the subject. Three years of working in the Alger Heights neighborhood had taught him all about Razi. He quickly washed his hands and began peeling the skin off the jicama, using the knife and cutting board Mama always left next to the soup pot.

"I haven't asked my alligator friends about jicama," Mr. Sanders said, slicing off a piece and holding it out to Keisha. "But next time they come by for a game of cards, I'll be sure to try it on them."

"We could ask ours, but we lost him," Razi informed Mr. Sanders. "He was taking a bath and then Grandma said 'Jumpin' Jimmy Choo' and then she said 'I could swear that door was closed' and then Mama and Daddy made us promise to stay in the kitchen and then—"

"Can baby Paulo try some jicama?" Keisha broke in, trying to redirect the conversation. She didn't think they should tell Mr. Sanders about the alligator. He liked to chat with all the neighbors, and it wouldn't look very good for Carters' Urban Rescue if people knew they'd caught the alligator in the city pool only to lose it in their house.

"Well, sure. I think he'd like jicama. It's sort of a cross between a water chestnut and an apple. But about this alligator—"

Razi had finally reached the packet on the counter. He grabbed it by the corner and held it out to Mr. Sanders. "Please open this for me. Please? I'll give you a marble. I'll give you a bottle cap."

"I'll help you, Razi." Keisha took it and tore it open. She didn't want him to trade away the baby. Last week, he'd offered baby Paulo to the grocery clerk for a Snickers bar. Besides, she wanted to get a good look at this whatever-it-was.

It was a plastic case, no bigger than a deck of playing cards, with a sticker on it that made it look like a music player. She could tell right away that if you pulled the ring on the string dangling from the case, it would play a song. This was a song she was about to become very familiar with. Keisha wondered if she'd like it.

Mr. Sanders put down his knife. "What I think you do, buddy, is pull on this string here. . . . Wait a minute . . . it's tangled. . . ."

While Mr. Sanders was messing with the toy, Keisha broke off a small piece of her jicama and put it in baby Paulo's mouth. She'd found this to be the very best way to test whether something was going to taste yucky. If babies didn't like something, they made a horrible face and spit it out. It was a fine thing to do if you were a baby, but it didn't go over very well when you were ten.

There was a great deal of clattering in the hall outside the kitchen, and Grandma was explaining to Daddy, "Of course the back door is latched. It was latched when I went out to water the primroses, and . . .

well, I latched it for sure the first time, but I had to go back out to scare the Zingermans' cat away from the bird feeder. That time, I can't be sure."

Baby Paulo, whose mouth had just been full of Cheerios a moment before, made an unhappy face, but he didn't spit out the jicama. This meant it might not be too bad. Keisha threw another handful of Cheerios on his tray and popped the rest of the jicama in her mouth.

"It tastes crunchy," she said, speaking loud enough to cover up the Grandma noises in the hall. "Mmmmm. You should try it, Razi."

But Razi was on the kitchen floor, full of concentration, trying to figure out how to untangle the string on the music player.

"I'll get the dog crate from the truck," Daddy was telling Mama. "Tell Mom to wait for me outside."

Keisha wished they wouldn't talk so loud.

Mr. Sanders resumed chopping his jicama and then stopped to look at Keisha. "This wouldn't have something to do with the alligator Mr. Ramsey found at the city pool this morning, would it?"

"Uhhhh . . ." Keisha was not nearly as good as Razi at making up stories. She looked at Mr. Sanders, wide-eyed, until baby Paulo started banging on his tray.

Ordinarily, Paulo was a mellow baby. Just watching

life unfold at Carters' Urban Rescue was interesting enough that he didn't need much more than to be fed and held and to have his diaper changed. But after Cheerios came yogurt, and every once in a while, the Carters got so busy that they forgot the yogurt part. So Paulo had to bang. If that didn't work, he had to fling anything that was within reach: his Winnie-the-Pooh bowl with the suction grip, his blue sippy cup, even his bib. Daddy said Paulo was going to be a pitcher for the Detroit Tigers, he had such a strong arm.

"Oops," Keisha said as Cheerios bounced off the baby's tray and onto the floor. "I forgot the yogurt."

She ran to the fridge, nearly tripping over Razi.

"Got it!" Razi said, and pulled the string. The room filled with the tinny sound of a tune you could hear on the radio up and down the block every day. It was from *Possum and Blossom,* a cartoon movie that Daddy had taken Keisha and Razi to last Saturday when it was raining.

The movie was about two possums and their life in the city. Very unrealistic if you knew the least little bit about possums.

"It's 'Possums in Love'!" Razi began to sing in a loud voice.

Keisha wondered how long the toy would last before it had an unfortunate accident. Or maybe she could convince her friend Aaliyah to trade Razi something for it. Aaliyah was very good at persuading.

"Mom, before you go out, can you see if we have any rats in the freezer downstairs?"

"Why do I always have to get the rats? It's hard to do those steps in high heels. Let Keisha do it."

"She's in the kitchen watching Razi and the baby!"

Keisha heard Grandma stomping down the basement stairs. A moment later, she heard the front door slam.

Mama rushed in from the hallway. She, too, almost tripped over Razi.

"Again!" Razi said, and yanked on the cord.

"Mr. Sanders . . . welcome." Mama stopped, took a deep breath and tugged on the hem of her shirt. "I see you smelled my soup."

"Yes, and I'm adding to it," Mr. Sanders said. He'd cut the jicama into matchstick-sized pieces and was dumping them into the pot. "So much going on here this morning . . ."

"Yes . . . yes." Keisha could tell that Mama's mind was also on alligators, not on chatting with Mr. Sanders. "So nice of you to stop by. Please eat as much soup as you like and take some home for Mrs. Sanders."

"I only have time for one small bowl."

Mr. Sanders knew where everything was. He pulled the ladle from the jug on the counter and a bowl from the cupboard above the sink.

"I always time my breaks for your house, as you know," he said, sipping his soup. "I've been here for twelve minutes, leaving me three more to eat this delicious soup." Mr. Sanders focused on slurping while Keisha and her mother exchanged glances.

"Mom, are you looking out here?" Daddy's voice was right outside the window.

Paulo's banging got louder.

"I keep forgetting the yogurt," Keisha said.

"I wish you could stay longer, Mr. Sanders, but I remember your motto: No rain or snow or soup can keep you from your appointed rounds." Mama took the empty bowl of soup from Mr. Sanders's hands and opened the back door.

"I see it! Right there. It's an alligator tail," Keisha heard Grandma say.

"That's the garden hose, Mom." Daddy had obviously reached the place where Grandma was standing.

"Actually, we don't have an official motto at the post office." Mr. Sanders was now leaning out the door, looking around the side of the house to see what

Grandma and Daddy were talking about. Keisha leaned outside for a look, too. "It was the Greek historian Herodotus who said: 'Neither snow, nor rain, nor heat, nor gloom of night stays these couriers from the swift completion of their appointed rounds.' He said that about twenty-five hundred years ago. It's on the New York City General Post Office, which was built in—"

"You have to admit it's the same color." Grandma was talking in her my-hearing-aid-isn't-quite-working voice.

"But alligators don't have spray nozzles on their tails."

"Very funny. I wasn't looking at that part. I was looking at the twisty part."

Mama gave Mr. Sanders a serious look before she said, "Good day, Mr. Sanders. We don't want to keep you from your appointed rounds, do we?"

With a little wave, Mr. Sanders was out the door, and Mama pushed it closed. Tight.

"Keisha, please give the baby his yogurt! And do not let anyone leave this room until we find that alligator!" Mama touched the tips of her long fingers to the place where her hair met her forehead. She always did this when she was thinking.

"We can't find it inside. Your father thinks the little

alligator will sniff for water, so we are going to look across the street where water collects by the drain. Muddy places. That is where the little alligator would go. I'm leaving Grandma in charge. Oh goodness . . ."

Mama got a wide-eyed look that Keisha had never seen before. She didn't say anything more before rushing back into the hall.

If Mama had given her just a minute, Keisha would have suggested taking Razi along. He was excellent at finding mud—messes of all kinds, really. But it was hard to think straight when the baby looked so unhappy. His bottom lip pushed out, Paulo was also tugging at his ear. If he started to rub his eyes, it would be too late. Paulo would have a meltdown. When Paulo had a meltdown, he cried for hours. Grandma said he could filibuster better than Senator Strom Thurmond. It had only happened three times in the history of the Carter family, but every baby had his limits. Keisha opened the refrigerator door again.

"Razi, can you please distract the baby while I get his yogurt?"

Razi jumped up. If there was one thing he was good at—besides finding mud—it was distracting. "Here, baby Paulo, listen to this." Razi dangled the music player over the tray.

But baby Paulo had had enough. He made a little howl, and before you could say "Mexican yam bean," he grabbed the music player and sidearmed it up and out the open window. It fell into the garden, still singing about sprinkling stardust sent from above over not one but two possums in love.

Chapter Five

Mr. Sanders did like to share information, so Keisha wasn't surprised at all when his twin boys, Zack and Zeke, appeared at the back door. Daddy had called them the Z-Team ever since they'd helped her out in first grade when her classmate Marcus knocked her down trying to steal the basketball at recess.

Zack and Zeke had rushed over. "We're big," Zeke said as he gave Keisha a hand up. "But we're sensitive, too."

Zack turned around and shook his fist at Marcus. "Try some of this if you can't stop pushing."

When Keisha told Daddy about what happened, he marched right over to the Sanderses' house to compliment the boys on their fine behavior, which included *not* punching Marcus. It was right about this time that Mr. Sanders started dropping off little packages for Razi.

It was like Mama said: "The bird who remembers his flock mates never misses the way."

Zeke and Zack looked exactly alike except that Zack had a chip in his front tooth from riding down Second Street shouting, "Ladies and gentlemen—no hands!"

Keisha opened the back door and pulled them into the kitchen.

Zack was the first to shout, "Where's the gator? We want to wrestle it."

Shouting wasn't good for baby Paulo's digestion.

Keisha *shhhhh*ed the boys and then whispered, "I think he's outside."

Zeke saw baby Paulo's unhappy look and went over to him. "Hey there, buster," he said, rubbing Paulo's cheek.

"Well, let's go, then." Zack grabbed the doorknob. "I don't want to be in here when all the action's outside."

Keisha had turned away from Paulo to talk to the boys, so her yogurt-filled spoon was heading in the wrong direction. Paulo started to yelp.

"Do you suppose my mama would let you hang around outside when there's an alligator on the loose?"

Zack let go of the doorknob and shoved his hands in his pockets. Even the Z-Team was a little afraid of Mama.

"True, but your grandma's out there. She keeps stepping on the garden hose."

"I think we should call the police and have the alligator arrested," Razi said. He'd taken the spoon from Keisha and was feeding the baby. Keisha let Razi take over because Razi was also good at feeding babies.

The phone rang.

"It's for me!" Razi dropped the spoon on the baby's tray.

Correction. Razi was good at feeding babies when there wasn't anything more interesting to do. Just like the mail, the phone was never for Razi, but he was always sure it was.

"Hello? Aaliyah? We can't talk right now because we have to call the police to get the alligator arrested."

"Razi!" Keisha was still whispering, though she knew there wasn't much point. "We're not supposed to *tell*."

"Uh-huh, uh-huh. Grandma let him out of the bathroom."

"Give me that." Keisha tried to grab the phone.

"Wait, we got cut off. . . ." Razi was punching buttons.

"Ouch!" Aaliyah was saying on the other end of the line. "You're making me deaf, Razi."

Zack quick picked Razi up and dangled him upside down. Zeke started to tickle him.

"Stop!" Razi was giggling. "Don't stop. No . . . stop!"

Razi dropped the phone, and Keisha almost lost her balance catching it. When she put the phone to her ear, she could hear Aaliyah laughing. "Sounds like you're playing hip-hopscotch. I better come over."

Aaliyah loved hip-hopscotch, which you played just like regular hopscotch, but you had to do a different dance move when you landed in each square.

"But I stop at alligators. You know I do not hop-scotch with alligators," Aaliyah said. "Key, do you really have one over there?"

Keisha wasn't sure what to say. "We did," she finally said. "We do. We just can't put our finger on him at the moment."

"So it's escaped. As in 'running wild in the neigh-borhood.'"

"Well, he *might* still be in the house."

"If it's true there's an alligator loose in Alger Heights, you know Moms is not going to let me outside this house. *Ever.* And it's almost summer vacation! How are we going to practice?"

Aaliyah spent the summer days at the house of her granny—whom everyone called Moms—while her parents were working. Even though it wasn't summer vacation yet, Aaliyah was spending the holiday weekend with Moms so her parents could attend their college reunion. Moms lived right around the corner from the Carters. Aaliyah's granny did not like dust, trouble or any animal whose stomach touched the ground when it moved. Mostly, that meant snakes, but now that Keisha thought about it, she decided that alligators would also qualify.

"Keisha, how are we going to win the Grand River Steppers Competition under-twelve category if you can't keep track of your alligators? And by the way, how can an alligator run around Michigan? It's way too cold here for alligators."

Aaliyah knew more about alligators than the average person because Keisha had asked her to read her alligator report for errors. Aaliyah did not forget the things she read. Aaliyah also thought too far ahead. They had not yet reached summer vacation, a time when Keisha, Aaliyah and their other best friend, Wen, had promised to spend time each day practicing their freestyle double Dutch. Winning the under-ten category last winter was easy, but now they had to compete against eleven-and-a-half-year-olds.

Keisha looked around her. Baby Paulo had put the yogurt bowl on his head, Zack was twirling Razi like an airplane and Razi was squealing with delight. Zeke was pouring Cheerios from the box into his mouth.

"Before I can think about alligators, I have to clean up this baby and find something for Razi to do."

"Until you catch that alligator, the rest of us can't go

outside to play. I'll get my binoculars and go up to the third floor. If I see anything long and suspicious, I'll call you."

"Sounds like a plan. And don't worry, Aaliyah. Mama and Daddy will find the alligator."

"Okay, I'll tell Moms that your mama's on it. She thinks your mama can do anything."

Keisha hung up the phone. First thing done. But what next? Whenever her mind was spinning from all the things that had to be done, Daddy would say to her, "What do you do if you're lost in the woods?"

What do you do if you're lost in the woods?

Stand still. The birds are not lost. The trees are not lost.

So Keisha stood still inside all the shouting and the movement and let the gears in her brain turn slowly. After one full minute, she whistled through her teeth the way Grandpa Wally Pops had taught her. Grandpa Wally Pops had been dead since Keisha was five, but Mama said his whistle was part of his memory line, the line that stretches from generation to generation and can never be broken.

A Grandpa Wally Pops whistle was short and sharp and shrill and it called everyone to attention.

"Since they already searched the house, I think it would be all right with Mama," Keisha said, looking at Zeke and Zack, "if you two take Razi upstairs and set up the train track."

"The train? Can I have my conductor's whistle?"

For obvious reasons, the Carters kept Razi's conductor's whistle in a secret place and only brought it out once in a while.

"Yes." Keisha told Zeke and Zack the current hiding

place. "If you boost Razi up, he can reach the top of the bookcase in Mama and Daddy's room."

"I can climb it myself like a monkey," Razi offered.

"The Z-Team is on it," Zeke said, very serious. He took Razi's top half.

Zack grabbed Razi's bottom half. "Chugga, chugga, chugga," Zack said.

"Woo-woo," Zeke answered back as they disappeared up the stairs. Keisha knew that even though Zack and Zeke were big kids now, they still liked to play with the toy train.

"Better keep the door closed," she said to their backs. Keisha thought of something else. "If you see any alligators," she called to them as they climbed the stairs, "no wrestling. Just tell me."

Keisha turned around and surveyed the kitchen. A chair was overturned. There were Cheerios on the floor, and baby Paulo had fallen asleep, his little legs dangling. One foot was missing a sock.

At least it was quiet. Keisha got down on her hands and knees and started to sweep the Cheerios into a pile. She put the cereal from the floor into the animals' dry-food container.

Paulo had licked the bowl clean before he put it on his head, so Keisha just got the counter sponge and slicked down his hair. She unlatched the tray, lifted Paulo out of the high chair and put him in his car seat. What was it about sleeping babies that made them three times heavier? Buckling him into his car seat on the counter, Keisha made sure Paulo's arms and legs were comfy.

Now that it was quiet, she could finally get down to some serious thinking. Pressing each of Paulo's toes in turn between her fingers, she whispered, "This little piggy goes to market, this little piggy stays home. . . ."

Counting baby toes, as everyone knows, is a wonderful way to settle down.

Keisha needed to settle down to figure out where a scared little alligator would go when he escaped from a bathtub. If he was frightened, he probably wouldn't go in the direction of the animal enclosures behind the

house. Too many noises and strange sounds and smells. While she was stroking the curve of baby Paulo's foot, a word popped into Keisha's brain—"moist." That's what the alligator would seek. His little osteoderms—those bony lumps under his scales—would want water. Alligators can smell water, too. Hadn't they found him in the city pool in the first place?

Just as Keisha was reaching her deepest and most excellent thinking-like-an-alligator thoughts, she was interrupted by the sound of a familiar song. Ugh. Even though she could barely hear it, she knew that song. It was "Possums in Love," the silly song on the music toy that Mr. Sanders had given Razi.

If Paulo hadn't thrown it out the window, Keisha could have pulled on the string until it broke so she'd have a little peace and quiet again.

Wait a minute.

Keisha froze, listening for the direction of the music. Baby Paulo had thrown the toy out the window over the sink. But the music was coming from the big window by the table. That was around the corner from where Paulo had thrown it.

How did the toy get around the corner? And *who* kept pulling the string?

Surely not an alligator!

Chapter Six

Keisha climbed onto the counter to stick her head out the open window. Looking to her right, Keisha could see Grandma across the alley, talking to Mr. Perkins about his sweet peas. She couldn't call out to her because at the corner of the house, she saw that the bushes were rustling! She could barely hear it, but wasn't that possum music in the bushes? And it was getting farther and farther away!

Keisha pulled her head back inside and sat on the counter. If only she could run outside and investigate, but Mama had said no one was to go outside—no exceptions.

She put her fingers at the place where her hair met her forehead. Maybe the noise was coming from someone's car and they were driving away. No, because a car driving would make the music disappear altogether, and Keisha could still hear the song. Hmmm. Maybe someone was playing it on their radio. No again. Because Keisha heard just the music and not the lady's voice like they had on the radio.

Keisha started rocking Paulo's car seat on the

counter next to her. Could the alligator have found the music toy and eaten it? That would explain how it moved! Everyone knows that the places things come out are not as big as the places things go in . . . especially with an alligator. Oh dear. They might have a very sick alligator on their hands. Keisha had to act quickly.

Every once in a while—not so very often—Keisha broke the rules. Daddy called it the gray area. It might be wrong, but if it was wrong for the right reasons, especially if it was an emergency, it was okay to break the rules.

Mama had been clear that Keisha was *not* to go outside. She was not to let anyone else outside, either. But Keisha could not think of another answer for how that toy moved around the house. There weren't any kids playing nearby. Razi was upstairs.

The question to ask was: Does an alligator swallowing a music toy make an emergency?

It might not if you were a normal person, but Keisha was part of Carters' Urban Rescue and *that* meant it *was* an emergency.

Keisha looked down at the sleeping baby. His head had fallen to the side, and bubbles of spit were coming out of his mouth. Tearing a piece of paper towel from the roll, Keisha wiped the spit bubbles away. She thought about running over to get Grandma, but Grandma didn't always help matters.

If the sound of the music was moving because the alligator ate the music toy, *then* wherever the music was the alligator was, and *if* she knew where the alligator was, *then* she could catch him.

But why was the alligator moving at all? In Keisha's experience, when animals were afraid, they stayed very still. If the alligator was under the bushes, he should be happy because the bushes would make him feel protected.

Wait. It was also very dry under the bushes. Keisha had been under those bushes to get the basketball, the Frisbee and Razi's Sunday school shoes. Every time she came out from under the bushes, Mama scolded her for getting her clothes dirty.

That's why the alligator was moving!

Under the bushes was very dry. Getting to wet was bigger than being scared. And Keisha knew if the alligator kept going around the house, he would find the very best spot of all for alligators at Carters' Urban Rescue: the muddy place by the hose.

Alligators like muddy places. The low place an alligator makes in the sand by digging and rolling is called a wallow. The rains come and fill the wallow with water and make it a soft and cool place for the alligator to lie when it gets hot.

If she was right and she had located the alligator, Keisha had a whole new set of questions: How do you catch an alligator if he can sense you coming from every side? What exactly do you catch the alligator with? And if you do manage to catch him, how do you keep him from escaping again before Mama and Daddy come home?

After four more "this-little-piggy's" on Paulo's toes, Keisha had an idea. It looked like this:

① Daddy's favorite game to play as a kid: Mousetrap, where you try to get someone else's mouse in a place where a basket falls on top and traps it.

② Z-Team

③ Z-Team belts

④ Picture window

⑤ LARGE laundry basket

⑥ 10-year-old weighing 55 pounds

⑦ Razi distracted

⑧ Paulo sleeping for 15 more minutes

Keisha climbed down off the counter and crept along the wall until she reached the picture window by the table. Yes! The music had turned the corner and was now moving toward her. And it had to pass under the window to get to the hose.

She ran upstairs, thinking that distracting Razi would be the hardest part of her plan.

"Oh no! Not another train off the cliff," Razi was saying as he pushed his engine over the side of the bed.

"Yes, yes. Here's the ambulance." Zeke pushed a red and white wagon toward the pile of crashed engines.

"Z-Team, I need your belts! And I need you to get the big laundry basket from under the chute in the basement. Put all the dirty laundry on top of the washer. Razi, you go in Mama's closet and get the flannel sheets. Just lay them out on the floor, okay? We're going to roll up that alligator like a bug in a rug."

"You said it again!" Razi shouted at the top of his lungs. He was already worked up from the train emergencies. "You're a poet and you didn't know it!"

"Yes, I am." Keisha turned around and ran back downstairs before her little brother could say any more. She had no plan to wrap the alligator in flannel sheets. That would make the little guy drier than he already was. Her plan was to wrap Razi in flannel sheets. Razi loved flannel sheets so much he would not be able to resist wrapping *himself* inside them, which might give her at least three minutes to capture the musical alligator.

The Z-Team met Keisha in the kitchen. They were panting from running down the stairs and then up from the basement.

"Can you help me get this window all the way open?" Keisha asked Zack. "Take a deep breath. We have to be quiet."

"You better fill us in," Zack said, "so we aren't at cross-purposes."

Mr. Sanders often said that when Zeke and Zack performed their chores, they were at cross-purposes. Take raking leaves, for example. If Zeke was raking and Zack was jumping in the pile, then the work wasn't getting done.

"We have to push together to get this big window all the way open because it sticks. Together, I think we can do it."

"That's clear enough," Zeke said, taking a position by the left side of the window. He started right in, tugging on the metal handle at the bottom of the frame.

"Roger that," Zack said, grabbing the windowsill.

With one big heave, the window was unstuck and opened wide. Lucky for Keisha, with all the raccoon cubs arriving last week, Daddy hadn't had a chance to put in the screen yet.

"Now take off your belts."

"What?" Zeke and Zack didn't like this part of the plan. They felt very protective of their belts with the Wild 4-Ever buckles they had earned after two years in their 4-H Club.

"She's going to beat it into the laundry basket," Zack said. "I'm horrified."

"No, she's going to buckle it in," Zeke said. "Does alligator slime come off leather?"

Keisha glanced out the window. The bushes were still rustling. The alligator was coming closer.

"Pay attention!" she whispered. "I'm not going to do either one of those things. Before Razi gets tired of those sheets upstairs, we have to get this done. I can't explain it all now, but if you want to be heroes, you'll pay attention."

Both Daddy and Mr. Sanders told the children that in times of crisis, heroes calmed down and worked together.

"I thought heroes calmed down and assessed the situation," Zeke said, taking off his belt.

"Well, yes, but I've already done that. In just a minute, I'm going to run outside and stand behind that horse chestnut tree. Turn the basket upside down and put your belts through the holes in the basket. The buckles will keep them from sliding all the way through. When I give you the sign, I want you to lower the basket onto the bushes. If it works, you'll trap the alligator."

"Holy smokes," Zack said, leaning out the window. "This feels like something on Animal Planet."

Keisha tugged on Zack's shirt. "Well, it won't if you keep hollering. Just stay quiet, okay? And listen for the music."

"The alligator sings?"

"Guys!" Keisha pointed at her eyes with her fingers in a V. Then she pointed at Zeke's, then at Zack's. It was what their fourth-grade teacher, Mrs. Norman, did when she wanted kids to listen up. "Try to stay focused and wait for my sign."

"What kind of sign will it be?" Zeke was sticking the end of his belt through a slot in the laundry basket. "A secret sign?" He liked spy signs.

"Nope. I'm just going to wave my hand. But I'd better hurry."

Keisha dashed out of the house and around the

edges of the yard until she ended up behind the tree. She was just about to wave to Zeke and Zack to let them know she was there, but then she realized they might think she was saying *Go!*

She could see Zack working his belt through the basket, but from her place on the ground, she could no longer see the bushes wiggling. They didn't seem to be moving now, but she *could* hear that music.

Zack poked his head out the window and turned so his ear was closer to the ground. Keisha could tell by the look on his face that he could hear it, too.

Zeke pushed the top of the basket out the window. It looked like he might drop it—or even drop out himself if he leaned any farther.

Keisha waved to get their attention. Then she gave the thumbs-up sign. She wanted to yell *Now!* but she was afraid she'd scare the alligator.

"Keisha girl!" Grandma called from across the alley. "What are you doing out in the sun without protection? I want grandchildren, not raisins!"

"Oh hush, Grandma," Keisha said under her breath. "C'mon, c'mon."

The laundry basket popped all the way out the window. The boys were lowering it, just like in Mousetrap!

As with all big moments that later turn into

exciting stories, everything seemed to occur at the same time. Keisha was sure she saw a flash of tail, Grandma crossed the alley without looking both ways and Mama and Daddy came around the side of the house. At the same time, Razi started screaming like crazy that he was stuck in the flannel sheets, and Keisha ran over to the basket and pressed it to the ground, pinning down a yew branch and something underneath it that she very much hoped was an alligator. She knew it was something alive because it made a sad little howl that sounded like *Yawk!*

A tail was sticking out from under the edge of the basket. Keisha lifted the edge just a bit so she could push the tail back under. Then she jumped on top of the basket and sat cross-legged just to make sure this crafty alligator couldn't escape again.

Yawk! He sounded very sad. Keisha bet that he wanted his mother. Poor thing. It reminded her of the way the rescued puppies at the pet-food store whimpered and howled, hoping someone would take them home. Just like the Razi sounds that were coming from the bedroom.

"Sweet." Zack and Zeke were hanging over the window ledge, watching. "Can we come down now and see him?"

"I told you it was right here," Grandma said, out of breath. "Why doesn't anybody ever listen to me?"

Chapter Seven

Mama called out to Keisha.

Keisha looked at Zeke, who was better at remembering directions. "First, take Paulo upstairs and put him in his crib. Then unroll Razi and put the sheets in the dirty laundry, *and then* . . ." She was going to tell them to put their belts back on, but the buckles were stuck inside the basket, so that would have to wait.

Normally, two ten-year-old boys might not listen to directions when there was an alligator sighting, but Zeke and Zack heard Mama's voice, too. They ran upstairs.

"Mama, Daddy, over here!" Keisha waved her arms. "I think I got it."

"Gracious heavens," Mama said when they reached Keisha. "What is my new laundry basket doing in all this dirt?"

Daddy squatted down. "Well, I see one dirty alligator underneath it, ready for a bath."

"Why do they keep playing that same song on the radio?" Grandma wanted to know. "Frankly, I'm sick of it."

"It's not the radio, Grandma," Keisha said as the last strains of "Possums in Love" died away. "It's the cereal toy Mr. Sanders gave Razi. You pull on a string and then it plays until the string goes back inside. Baby Paulo threw it out the window, and the way the music kept moving around, I was afraid the alligator had swallowed it."

Keisha leaned over and looked through the plastic slots of the laundry basket. The little alligator was moving its head back and forth as if it were saying to Keisha, *No music toy in here.*

"Keisha, my girl," Mama said, "you need to come away from that alligator. Even baby alligators can bite off fingers and toes."

Keisha peered through the slots once again. The alligator was still shaking its head. She just *had* to solve this mystery.

"The music doesn't play for very long and then you have to pull the string again. But if he'd swallowd it, the alligator couldn't have been pulling the string. So how did the music keep playing? And why has it stopped now?"

"I missed a chapter," Grandma said. "But if you have the alligator, then I suggest we rummage through the cupboards and find something for dinner. I'm starving."

Grandma was always starving.

"Maybe we could make s'mores tonight," she suggested. "In honor of the Great Alligator Hunt."

Grandma was always thinking of excuses to make s'mores, her favorite dessert. But Keisha was not going to be distracted—even by the promise of s'mores. This was a puzzle and she was trying to put the pieces together. The music stopped when they dropped the basket. Was that a coincidence, or . . .

Of course. That was it! When an alligator moves, most of it goes on the ground. Some part of the alligator must have gotten stuck on some part of the music player—maybe the little ring used to pull the string—and dragged it along.

"Mama, Daddy, that music player is in here somewhere. Some part of it is stuck on some part of our alligator."

"Stuck on *the* alligator," Mama corrected Keisha. "This is not our alligator, Key." Mama pulled up her skirt so she could kneel on the grass and look in herself.

"Fred," Mama said after squinting at the alligator

for a long time, "do you know what this child is talk-ing about?"

Daddy squatted down next to Mama. "No, Fay, I don't. But like most things, the answers will be revealed in the bath."

"The bathtub with the new ena—"

"I want to see the alligator. Please!" Freed from the sheets, Razi had picked up speed coming down the stairs and out the back door.

He was about to launch himself onto the laundry basket when Daddy snatched him up. "Whoa, buddy."

The Z-Team followed close behind, panting.

"He's slippery," Zeke said, tucking his shirt back into his pants.

"Squirmy's more like it," added Zack.

"Move back, guys," Daddy said, drawing the boys away from the laundry basket.

"If we get down on our knees and crawl over slowly, can we look at it?"

"What is sticking out of that basket?" Grandma asked.

"Our Wild 4-Ever belts," Zeke and Zack said in one voice.

Zack was bent double, peering into the basket. "If you're gonna eat one of those belts, Ally, could you eat the one by your tail? That's my brother's."

"Nobody's going to eat anything. . . . Well . . ."
Daddy rubbed his tummy. Like Grandma, he was always
hungry. "Not any Wild 4-Ever belts, anyway. All the
boys need to go back in the house. This alligator has
had enough excitement for one day without a bunch of
strangers staring at him."

Keisha watched Daddy pass a squirming Razi over to
the Sanders twins.

"I'm thinking maybe the dog crate and then back
into the bathtub," Daddy said, glancing over at Mama.

Mama frowned, thinking. "What we need for this
alligator is a wallow."

Razi stopped squirming. "What's a wallow?" he
asked. "Do I want one?"

"Yes," Keisha sighed. "You do, but you're not going
to get one. In the wild, alligators make wallows all by
themselves. They roll around until there's . . . Well, it's
like a hole and then it fills with water."

"And then?"

"And then it keeps the alligator moist. *And
then* . . . ," she continued, remembering, "other animals
and insects use it, too, even when the alligator moves
on, so wallows are an important part of the marshland."

Razi couldn't help it. He had to keep going. "And
then the alligators give their wallow to the insects and

then everybody has a going-away party and then the alligators cry and pack their suitcases and then they get on the wrong bus and go to Michigan and then they end up in the city pool and then—"

Razi managed to distract Zeke and Zack enough with his story to squiggle free.

"He's breached security!" Zack shouted as Razi tried to get away. But Daddy was ready. He turned Razi upside down, held him by the ankles and blew raspberries on his tummy.

"I wish I had some of his energy," Grandma said. "I need a protein bar."

Mama sighed. "Back in my bathtub with the new enamel."

"Let's buy a wallow, Daddy," Razi said between giggles. "I like that word 'wallow.' Wallowwallowwallowwallow—"

Daddy paused from blowing raspberries on Razi's stomach. "You can't buy a wallow like you can a wading pool, Razi. It's like Keisha said. Alligators make their own."

"This alligator needs to be in the zoo," Grandma said. "Whoever heard of an alligator in a bathtub?"

"There's an alligator in the house on East Eighty-eighth Street," Razi said between giggles.

"That was a crocodile, Razi," Keisha reminded her brother. "And the zoo offices don't open until Tuesday, Grandma."

"Well," Grandma said, curling some stray hairs back behind her ear. "I think we should bring back the no-reptiles-allowed rule."

There had never been a no-reptiles-allowed rule at Carters' Urban Rescue, but Grandma had voted for one at family meetings when she'd been bitten on the knuckle by a box turtle.

"Maybe we should get him a wading pool, Mama," Keisha suggested.

"I don't think so." Mama made the *tsk*ing sound with her tongue that meant something wasn't right with the world. "The poor thing wouldn't get any peace. Every child in the neighborhood and most of the grown-ups would want to see it.

"No, no," she continued. "This is not an exhibit. I am afraid the little one goes back into the bathtub. Daddy will put an old piece of carpet in the bottom so it can't scratch my new enamel."

Mama took Razi from Daddy. He didn't struggle so much in her arms. He put his head on her shoulder as she followed behind Grandma.

"I want to see an alligator hole, Mommy." Razi

rubbed his forehead against Mama's shoulder. "I want to see a wallowwallowwallow."

Daddy pulled the hose over to where Keisha sat on the basket. He placed the hose on the ground nearby so the water could seep in. He turned on the nozzle just a trickle. "It's a good thing this hose has been sitting in the sun. The water will be nice and warm."

Keisha felt a shift underneath the basket.

"Why don't you lie down on your tummy," Daddy suggested. "Then you can see him. He can't hurt you under the basket. I think he's just trying to get comfortable.

"Now tell me about how you found this alligator." Daddy started to lie down on his stomach, too, to get a better view. He was sure to get wet that way, but Daddy didn't care about those things.

"What's this?" He reached out and pulled the little music player from underneath the edge of the basket.

"That's it!" Keisha took the music player from her father. It was cracked down the middle.

"This is what I think," Keisha said, trying to remember. "When baby Paulo threw the toy out the window, it landed under the bushes. The alligator saw the shiny ring and bit at it . . . or maybe it got stuck on one of the parts of him that drag on the ground—"

Keisha stopped for a minute and put her hands over her eyes. She was trying to picture it. "When I heard the music from a different spot, I was worried that the alligator had swallowed the whole toy. I was afraid he would choke, but then I realized the music was too loud to be inside an alligator. The only explanation was that the little alligator was somehow pulling the string. If the ring was around his tooth or his toenail, then he would keep dragging the toy and pulling the string and the music would play. Right?"

Daddy looked up at the window. His eyes followed the path along the house that the alligator had taken. Then he looked up at the window again.

"You must have broken it when you jumped on the basket," Daddy said, examining the cracked toy and the frayed string.

He added, "Even if he ate the plastic ring and the string, I don't think that would be too much of a danger. Alligators eat all sorts of things. Still, I'd better get him out of here and into the dog crate and see if I can find the rest of the string. When the zoo offices open on Tuesday, we'll take him in to Mr. Malone, who handles all the reptiles there. He'll give the little guy a checkup."

"Can he stay here for just a minute?" Keisha was watching the alligator push his snout into the dirt.

Could he smell the water seeping up through the ground? "He deserves a little rest and relaxation."

"Well, one more minute wouldn't hurt." Daddy patted Keisha's back. Then he smiled. "After we give this alligator a bath, Miss Keisha, would you like to play a game of Mousetrap?"

Chapter Eight

Keisha wasn't sure why keys were so big in the old days, but the good part was that big keys made big keyholes in old houses, and big keyholes meant that you could let your two best friends look into the bathroom at an alligator without breaking your promise to *not* let your friends into the bathroom to look at an alligator.

"He's not that big," Aaliyah said. Aaliyah was the tallest of the three of them, with broad shoulders, deep brown eyes and always the newest and prettiest hairstyles because her grandma braided hair for just about everyone in Alger Heights.

"But *you* are," Wen said. She was hopping up and down, trying to see over Aaliyah's shoulder. Wen was the shortest of the three. She had the shortest hair, too, and always the highest kneesocks during the school year. Wen went third in double Dutch practice because when your arms are tired, you want someone small to swing the ropes for. Plus, Wen was graceful. She almost never messed up on motions.

Razi burst into the hall and pushed both girls aside. "Let me see."

"Razi! You've already seen the alligator. At the pool. These are our guests."

"Did not." Razi stuck out his bottom lip and pressed his face to the door. "He was moving too fast. I want to see him standing still." Razi pulled away from the key-hole. "Now he's asleep. That's boring."

"I don't think he's asleep," Keisha said, forgetting about the guests herself and pressing her face to the door. "I think he's still frozen with fear. Imagine all the places this poor alligator has been today. He'd be so much happier tucked into a muddy wallow, up to his snout in mud."

"Wait . . . don't tell me. . . ." Aaliyah stood still, remembering. "A wallow . . ."

"Let me say. Let me say it!" Razi's voice rose in excitement.

Keisha clapped her hand over his mouth. "You're going to scare the poor thing to death," she said.

Razi broke away and ran down the stairs. "I'm gonna tell Mama. You almost stuffocated me!"

While all this was going on, Wen was examining the alligator through the keyhole. "He is small," she said. "Maybe he's a Chinese alligator."

"I didn't know there were alligators in China," Keisha said. Secretly, she thought she knew everything there was to know about alligators. But this was news to her. "How can you tell?" Keisha asked Wen.

Wen shrugged.

"Speak Chinese to him . . . duh." Aaliyah turned to face the girls, flipping her braids so that they clicked like a bunch of chopsticks falling into a bowl.

"What should I say?" Wen wanted to know.

"Sing something," Keisha said. "A lullaby. That lullaby you sing in Chinese is so pretty."

Wen's grandmother, Nei-Nei, was always singing to her. Keisha loved to listen.

"Okay. I will sing 'Rock-a-bye, rock-a-bye, sleep now, you're safe with me,'" Wen decided. "*Yao-yao-yao, yao-yao-yao, xiao bao bao, kuai shui jiao. . . .*"

Wen's voice was very soft and high when she sang. It sounded to Keisha like the wind when it goes through the tops of the trees in Riverside Park.

"Nope," Aaliyah said, keeping watch as Wen finished her song. "He didn't even wave his tail, but I do hear something. . . ." She pulled her head away from the door and turned to listen. "You must have left the hose running," she said. "I can hear it."

Everyone was quiet for a moment. When the water was on, you could often hear it rattling through the pipes of the old house. Keisha looked through the keyhole. She was sure Daddy had turned off the tap before he went downstairs. Still, water was running somewhere.

Keisha went into her bedroom so she could see down to the backyard where they'd left the hose. From the window, she saw her brother lying down, rolling back and forth in the bare spot beneath the horse chestnut tree. Usually, that spot was filled with dirt, but now it was mud because the hose *was* on and water was spurting from the nozzle.

Keisha pushed the window open. "Razi Carter! *What* are you doing? Mama's gonna kill you!"

"I'm making a wallow for the alligator," Razi shouted back. He did not stop rolling.

"Oh, Razi. When Mama sees this—" Keisha pulled her head back into the house. Mama would be mad at *her* for this. She was supposed to be watching Razi. How could a girl be expected to watch Razi and make sure an alligator didn't escape from the bathroom at the same time?

She pushed her head back out of the window. "You're all muddy," she yelled at Razi.

"It's how the alligators do it," he yelled back. "You said."

Suddenly he sat up. "I got dirt in my eyes." He began to rub and rub.

"Don't rub!" she called down to her brother. "I'll be right there."

Keisha knew that if she didn't rescue Razi from this situation, he would have not only the sting of dirt in his eyes but also a lecture that included several wise Nigerian sayings like "He who digs a pit for others is just as likely to fall into it himself."

She rushed back to Wen and Aaliyah, who had figured out a way they could both see through the keyhole at the same time by pressing their heads together.

"He doesn't look good," Wen said. "Maybe he's hungry."

"Mama and Daddy are out buying food," Keisha told them. "But I've got another emergency. Will you two make sure this door stays closed?"

Wen and Aaliyah locked arms. "We will," Aaliyah said.

When Keisha got outside, water was gushing from the hose—oooh, that would make Mama angry, too!— and Razi was still crying over the dirt in his eyes. He wasn't making it any better, either, by rubbing his face with his dirty hands.

"Razi. Hold still. I can't help you if I can't look at what is hurting."

Razi stopped for a moment and covered his eyes with the palms of his hands. Then he started in again. Keisha rolled up her pants and kneeled down next to Razi. She reached out for his hand.

"You're still rubbing it in."

"I know!" Razi said, pulling away from her and crying some more.

Keisha sat back. Every older sister had her limits. Wrestling with her brother in a muddy gator hole was not something Keisha Carter was willing to do.

She'd have to figure out another way. Keisha stood up and ran over to the shed, where they kept the gardening tools. She rooted around in a pile of seed-starting trays and tulip-bulb food because she knew it was over here somewhere. Yes! The spray nozzle.

Razi loved the spray nozzle. Mama didn't let him play with water too much, but when she watered the vegetable patch, she let Razi stand with one foot on either side of the okra row holding an umbrella. That way, he could pretend it was raining and her plants still got watered.

Keisha turned off the water, ran back to her brother and waved the spray nozzle. "Look what I've got!" She attached it to the end of the hose and turned the water back on, all to the tune of unhappy Razi's crying.

But when she pressed the handle and a fountain of soft rain began to fall on Razi's head, he stopped rubbing his eyes and put his hand out to catch the rain.

"Instead of being an alligator, you can be Lyle, Lyle, Crocodile," Keisha said. "This is your first shower."

"I go in the shower with Daddy," Razi said, tipping his head up to taste the rain. "When I'm six, I can go in by myself."

"When you're six and you can hold the soap without dropping it . . . and when you can take all your clothes off by yourself." She moved the nozzle so it was aimed at the back of Razi's shirt.

"I can take my clothes off by myself!"

"Not when they're wet you can't."

"Can."

"Prove it. I dare you."

A dare was one of the few situations where Razi could focus his whole self, from his fingers to his toes. Razi loved to win a dare. Before you could say "Ollie Ollie Oxen Free," he was down to his underwear and struggling to unlace his sneakers.

Wen called out from the open window, "The baby's crying. Should I get him up?"

"Yes, but make Aaliyah promise to stay by the bathroom door."

"Okay. No Grandma sightings yet."

Keisha rinsed out Razi's muddy clothes while her brother danced like a prizefighter around the horse chestnut tree. "He did it, ladies and gentlemen." Razi thumped his chest. "He won the double dare!"

Wasn't a double dare, Keisha almost said out loud.

Wen appeared on the back steps, with Paulo in her arms, just as Mama and Daddy pulled into the garage.

"We have frogsicles," Daddy said, holding up a bag of frozen frog parts.

"And chicken." Mama climbed out and took in the mess around her: her son twirling around the tree in his underwear, the muddy patch beneath their feet, the running water and Wen struggling down the steps with baby Paulo. Mama took the sleepy baby and cradled him in her arms.

"Just don't tell me that Grandma is watching that alligator," she said in her calm Mama voice.

"No, Mama. Aaliyah is watching the alligator, and Grandma is upstairs lying down with a wet washcloth over her eyes."

Mama cupped Keisha's chin in her free hand. "Keisha, my girl, I know there is a good story—"

"I'm Lyle, Lyle, Crocodile and I just had my first shower. Keisha double-dared me to take my clothes off and I won!" Razi raced around the tree again, waving his fists in the air.

Keisha looked up at her mama. What could she add to that?

Chapter Nine

The next morning, a CFC was held at the kitchen table. Grandma was in her new bathrobe made of organic hemp. She had two of Keisha's plastic butterfly barrettes on the lapel and was wearing the pink headband that made her eyes look more lifted, though Keisha still wasn't sure how that worked. Razi was underneath the table in his superhero pajamas, eating graham crackers spread over a napkin. Daddy had given him a set of old lug nuts, and he was picking them up with a super-sized magnet.

"I'm concerned about this alligator," Daddy said, putting peanut butter on a cracker and handing it to the baby. "The little guy seems listless."

"What's 'listless'?" Keisha wanted to know.

"He's got no get-up-and-go," Grandma said.

"Isn't that good?" Razi asked from under the table. "He had some of that yesterday, and it made a lot of crisis for everybody."

"Well, I think he needs a checkup."

"It's Memorial Day, Mom. Nobody's open. I've got a call in to Dan Malone at the zoo, but we'll have to wait until Tuesday."

Mama was at the stove finishing the corn porridge. "I looked in on the little one this morning, Fred. You're right. It seems too quiet."

"We need a house call." Grandma took the bowl Mama handed her. "Keisha, be Grandma's best girl and get me the sweet milk."

Keisha got the can of sweetened evaporated milk from the fridge.

"Mom," Daddy said, spooning porridge into his mouth, "how do you get a house call when the offices are closed?"

Grandma reached into the pocket of her fluffy bathrobe and pulled out her cell phone. "I have Dan's cell phone in my directory. I put him on speed dial after I had that run-in with the box turtle."

Grandma didn't ask the other Carters if they thought it was a good idea to bother Dan Malone on a holiday weekend. She simply put on her reading glasses and punched in the number.

"Dan? Is that you? I didn't wake you up, did I? You're where? At the cemetery? Well, I guess that makes sense. They don't call it Memorial Day for nothing. The problem is, Dan, we've got an alligator emergency on our hands. . . ."

Grandma didn't mess around. As it turned out,

Dan's grandfather, a World War II veteran whose grave Dan was decorating for the holiday, was in a cemetery not far from the Carters' house. Dan Malone would make a house call.

"Ask and ye shall receive." Grandma flipped her phone shut. "He'll be here in fifteen minutes." She patted her robe. "Heavens to Betsey Johnson!" Grandma exclaimed. "I better get dressed."

She took one last bite of her porridge. "Here, Keisha, finish mine. You can use some meat on those bones."

"Well, that's a new development," Daddy said as Grandma hurried past. "So much for a CFC."

"I'm glad," Mama said. "That little one is not right."

"Maybe you should give him some graham crackers," Razi said. "You can mix them with sweet milk and make them mushy like you do for Paulo."

"Maybe . . ." Mama dished out another bowl for Daddy, handed Keisha a spoon and passed her Grandma's bowl. "Maybe Dan will want some porridge."

There was a knock at the back door. "We had breakfast," Zack said, pushing the door open before anyone could answer it. "But we still haven't seen the alligator up close."

"Me either!" Razi ran up to Zeke and did the high-five-low-five-slide handshake the boys had taught him. "Only Keisha and Daddy have."

"Is it a girl alligator or a boy alligator?" Zack asked.

"How can you tell?" Zeke wondered.

Keisha wasn't sure how to tell, but she didn't want Zeke and Zack to know that. "I couldn't really see with the alligator in the laundry basket." She reached for the honey. "What difference does it make?"

"How can you name an alligator unless you know if it's a boy or a girl?" Zack intercepted the honey and squirted some on his finger.

"Pumpkin," Razi said, hopping up and down, nearly upsetting Mama's bowl. "That's his name! I vote for Pumpkin." Razi waved his hand wildly. "Who votes for Pumpkin?"

"Too much energy in my kitchen," Mama said. "We'll wait for Mr. Malone. Razi, you can take the boys up to look through the keyhole. But be quiet. That little gator is frightened enough already."

"Will you give me a piggyback ride?" Razi asked

Zeke. Razi always asked Zeke first because he hardly ever said no. "Please?"

Almost as soon as they were gone, Mr. Malone came to the back door.

"It's the alligator doctor," Daddy said, "here to charge us double overtime for making a house call on a holiday."

"Got my doctor's kit and everything," Mr. Malone said, holding up a little suitcase. "Never know what I'll come across at the side of the road."

"We appreciate it, Dan." Mama was already up and headed toward the pot on the stove. "Can I get you some—"

"No, you sit, Fayola. I always take Mom to breakfast after church on Memorial Day weekend. I'm stuffed. How big did you say this alligator was?"

Daddy looked at Keisha.

"Three bread boxes and a tail," she told him. "Or one rescue tube."

Mr. Malone looked thoughtful. "I'll probably need two assistants to help me examine it," he said, glancing at Daddy. "Might be best to have one big one and one little one."

"I could be the little one," Keisha offered. She pulled Daddy's hand onto the table and put hers next to it.

"You want *Keisha* to work on this gator?" Mama asked.

"I could take the mouth, Fred the tail, and Keisha here could hold down the middle in case it tries to roll."

"I'm strong enough to hold it, Mama. See?" Keisha picked up the kitchen stool and pumped it over her head a few times.

Mama didn't have time to decide if pumping the stool up and down was proof enough that Keisha could hold down alligators because Grandma came bursting into the room, dressed in her purple Chinese-collared silk shirt.

"There's been a breach of security," she said. "I can't be expected to watch over the alligator *and* get ready for the day when—"

"Did the alligator get out?" Mama dropped her spoon.

"Don't get your knickers in a knot, Fay. I just caught the boys—" Grandma saw Mr. Malone. "Oh, hi there, Dan. Seen any vicious box turtles lately?"

"None as vicious as the one that got its teeth into you, Alice. That was the mother of all box turtles."

The boys came rushing in. "It was his fault!" Zeke said, pointing at Zack. "He almost took my head off slamming the door shut."

"You pushed me in there first."

"That was Razi."

"You dared me!" Razi screamed.

"Boys, boys! Take this outside." Daddy stood up and shooed the boys toward the door. "There must be some wholesome activity you can find to do while we conduct some business here."

"What's 'wholesome'?" Razi asked.

"Filled with holes," Zack said.

"Is not," Zeke said.

"Is so," Zack said back. It continued like that until they were outside.

"Shall we visit an alligator?" Mr. Malone asked.

"We shall." Daddy led the way upstairs. He held the bathroom door open for Mr. Malone and Keisha and then he closed it carefully. As soon as the alligator heard them enter, it began scrabbling against the tub bottom, trying to gain its footing and escape. In an instant, Mr. Malone was kneeling at the side of the claw-foot tub with his hands clamped around the alligator's mouth.

"Help me out here, guys. I had my jaw dislocated by an alligator's tail in graduate school."

Daddy kneeled down on one end, and Keisha took her place in the middle. Oooh, the alligator felt, well, like a bumpy old bicycle tire. He was softer than she thought he would be. As soon as their hands were in place, the poor little thing started twisting.

"The death roll," Mr. Malone said. "He's trying to get away. We'll sit him out. Just hold." The alligator did try, but he didn't seem to have much energy for it. After a few seconds, he lay still.

"Don't let go, but relax," Mr. Malone told them. "We need to move him back so he's flat on the bottom of the tub."

Keeping one hand clamped on the alligator's mouth, Mr. Malone took a pen out of his shirt pocket and lifted the base of the alligator's tail. "I should say we need to move *her* to the bottom of the tub."

Mr. Malone leaned in close and inspected every inch of alligator.

"She has the typical scratches on her skin that an alligator would get when you chase her over the cement at the city pool. Let's see those eyes. . . . Keisha, would you get the magnifying glass out of my instrument case?"

Keisha snapped open Mr. Malone's case and laid it flat on the floor. It held everything from adhesive bandages to syringes to thermometers. She found the magnifying glass and looked at Pumpkin's eyes as she handed the glass to Mr. Malone. They looked like some of the specimens in her cat's-eye marble collection, deep brown with flecks of yellow.

"Excellent," Mr. Malone said. "No scratches there."

He set the magnifying glass down and used his free hand to pull back her lips so he could see her gums.

"Oh, this is not good."

"Are Pumpkin's teeth loose?" Keisha remembered something about alligator teeth in captivity, but she wasn't sure what.

"Pumpkin? That's an odd name for an alligator. I thought Fay—"

"Not her official name," Daddy said. "We try not to get too attached, but Razi has a way of naming everything."

Keisha wanted to hear what Mr. Malone thought about naming. Did they name the animals at the zoo? Did he think of one of them as his special pet? She kept her grip tight with one hand, but with the other, she patted Pumpkin's back.

"Her teeth aren't loose," Mr. Malone said, absorbed again in alligator anatomy, "so much as . . . transparent. Like skim milk. She is missing some teeth, too. And see here . . ."

He put one hand on top of Pumpkin's jaw and one

hand under it and moved the bottom from side to side. Ooooh, Pumpkin didn't like that. Daddy jumped back as her tail got away from him and smacked against the side of the tub.

Keisha squinted and ducked. Pumpkin struggled to get free, but Daddy got her tail again and they put pressure on her until she stopped fighting.

Everyone was breathing hard—especially Pumpkin—when Mr. Malone said, "She's a little sensitive here. It's just as I thought. She doesn't eat enough bones."

"Bones?" Daddy repeated.

Mr. Malone nodded. "Alligators in captivity are almost always fed a diet of things like hamburger and tuna and chicken without the bones. They need the whole animal: rats, mice, chicks. Otherwise, they don't get enough calcium.

"Before she was found in the city pool, it's likely that someone had her in their home—the garage or the basement—and fed her food that was easy to get at the grocery store. I've seen this before."

"So people do have alligators for pets?" Keisha asked.

"Sure they do." Mr. Malone straightened his back. "Think about this one as a baby—those glassy eyes, the smile that never goes away. They're like scaly kittens, just twelve inches long. Pretty hard *not* to want one."

Keisha tried to imagine Aaliyah begging her mama and daddy for a baby alligator. She wasn't sure Mr. Malone was right in thinking everyone wanted one.

"Did you ask for an alligator when you were little?" she asked him.

"You bet I did."

Keisha didn't ask her next questions—*Did you get one? How much did it cost? Where did you keep it? What happened when it got big?*—because she didn't want Daddy to think that she had any interest at all in baby alligators.

"Okay, everybody, on the count of three we're all going to stand up and back off. . . . One, two, three . . ." Keisha was the quickest to jump up. Daddy took her hand and pulled her away. She was sure the alligator would try to get out of the tub again. It had been successful once. But poor Pumpkin seemed exhausted.

"Let's make our getaway while we can," Daddy said. When they were on the other side of the bathroom door, Daddy tilted a chair from Grandma's bedroom up against the door to make sure it stayed shut.

"Maybe she could come live with you at the zoo," Keisha said as they were going down the stairs.

"I'm afraid not, Keisha. This alligator may have a virus, one we can't see, and we can't take the chance of her infecting others. Also, a zoo isn't set up to take in orphaned animals, like your dad does," Mr. Malone said. "We don't even have the proper licenses. . . ."

They walked into the kitchen, where Grandma was sitting at the table cutting pictures out of her Elder-hostel catalog.

Mr. Malone went to the kitchen sink to wash his hands. "There's another reason we can't take Pumpkin," he told Keisha over his shoulder. "The zoo doesn't have enough room. In the three years I have worked there, we've seen eight alligators—two just this month. The last one was caught with a fishing rod. It had made a wallow on the Rogue River and was eating the free-range chickens at the Herbruck family farm."

"But where do they come from? Michigan isn't an alligator's natural habitat," Keisha said.

"They aren't coming by themselves. People bring them. Or they buy them here. My parents knew what happened to baby alligators—that's why I never got one. But people who go to reptile swaps—they have one every month here in Grand River—don't know the first thing about it. They see the alligator while it's a hatchling, and they don't think ahead to the fact that alligators grow big and dangerous.

"Another thing I learned in my online zoo forum is that people are starting to use them the way they might use guard dogs. So instead of a pit bull, some property owners buy alligators."

"Does this mean there will be more and more alligators in Michigan?"

"Not in the end because they can't survive our Michigan winters."

"So what will happen to Pum—*this* alligator?"

"I'm sorry, Keisha." Daddy patted her back. "It's not looking too good for our scaly friend."

"Well, just think if you hadn't found her," Mr. Malone said. "How sick and frightened she'd be. Nature, as you know, Keisha, can be very cruel. I include human beings when I say that. No one should have released Pumpkin like that. Here in Michigan, she's like a . . . well, a fish out of water!"

Chapter Ten

The good news was that Pumpkin wasn't going back to Mama's favorite bathtub. The bad news was that Mama had to lose a flower bed. Daddy had warned her not to plant the petunias in that spot because they would need a large-animal enclosure soon. Mama said she'd rather give up the petunias than have an alligator back in the house. Daddy cut the flowers and put them in a vase. Then he dug out a whole section of earth, including the roots of the petunias so they could be planted elsewhere.

All the while, Keisha misted Pumpkin in the dog crate that had been placed in the shade outside the garage. Razi and Grandma stood on the other side, talking about what would happen.

"Shame about your mama's petunias," Grandma said, scratching at a scab on her knee. She was wearing her "skort," which made her legs look longer.

"That should be the alligator's new name." Razi pushed a flower between the slats of the crate. "Pumpkin is a boy's name, but Petunia is a girl's name."

The alligator snapped at the flower.

"Razi! We're supposed to keep her calm." Poor thing, Keisha thought. Alligators shouldn't have to be crammed into dog crates—or any other cage or aquarium that was too small—for too long. Besides, this little one had been through trouble enough. She deserved some rest.

Daddy walked over and Keisha reached up to wipe the dirt off his chin.

"Time for your nap, buddy." Technically, Razi was too old for his nap, but Daddy still made him go upstairs and play in his room when the family needed a rest.

"Is not!"

"Is. It is a quarter past naptime, to be exact. Grandma, will you read Razi a story?"

"Only if I can pick it. I've had it with stories about trains. I need more excitement than clickety-clack."

After the others left, Keisha tried to make her thoughts calm for the alligator's sake. She wondered what a reptile thought about. Did Pumpkin-Petunia feel better that Keisha was there?

The alligator *was* cute, like Mr. Malone said, in a scaly sort of way. Her eyes were following Keisha. She knew that what looked like Pumpkin-Petunia smiling was just the way her jaw was formed, but secretly Keisha felt that Pumpkin-Petunia, or whatever her name was, might be having some feelings for Keisha, too.

The alligator squiggled in her little space, swishing her tail back and forth. Keisha stroked the side of the crate. Pumpkin-Petunia snapped her jaws.

"Shhhh," Keisha said. "It's going to be all right. I'm your friend."

"Keisha, my lovely girl," Mama called from the window. "You have to wash your hands for dinner. I am making *egusi*."

Egusi was a spicy yellow soup made with meat, red chilies, ground dried shrimp, pumpkin and vegetables.

Mmmmmm. It was Keisha's favorite.

"And *chin-chin*."

Mmmm again. Keisha loved to dip the sweet fried *chin-chin* bread into her soup.

"Will Petunia be okay out here by herself?"

"I thought she was Pumpkin. . . . You know what your daddy thinks about naming the animals. . . ."

"She's Pumpkin-Petunia Carter," Keisha said quietly.

"We'll be right up here. I'll keep the window open so you can check. I need you to set the table. I invited Mr. Sanders and the twins."

"PetuniaPetuniaPetunia." Razi came running down the steps with a fistful of flowers. So much for his rest.

"She's Pumpkin-Petunia now," Keisha said. "You're holding those too tight. You're crushing the stems."

Razi took Keisha's mister and started to spray the flowers. They were already drooping. If only he could learn not to hold so tight.

"These need to be put in water, Razi. Come on. I'll be right back, Pumpkin-Petunia."

Inside, the kitchen was filled with the smell of fried *chin-chin*. Mama made the dough in the afternoon and fried up squares while grinding the pumpkin seeds and making the paste of onion, tomato and pepper for her *egusi* soup.

Baby Paulo had taken a long nap. His big brown eyes took in all the activity around him. Daddy was sitting next to the baby, and when Paulo was ready for another spoonful of mashed yams, he pounded the high chair a few times and then opened his mouth like a bird. Razi darted under the table with a set of keys and Daddy's toolbox.

Keisha washed her hands.

"I've got it!" Grandma said. She was waving a bunch of papers and almost walked right past her chair. Grandma had the oldest bones, so she got the chair with the biggest cushion.

"Got what?" Zeke asked, pushing open the back door.

"A place in Alabama that takes in lost alligators. I found it on the Internet."

Daddy rinsed the baby's dishes as Mr. Sanders and
Zack filed in behind Zeke. Keisha found the guest chair
from the living room so there were places for everyone.
It was Mrs. Sanders's Bunco night, so she would be out
late throwing dice with her friends.

"Are you sure it's not an alligator farm, Mom? There
are places that raise alligators for their meat and skins,
you know."

Daddy spooned out the soup. Zeke and Zack didn't like *egusi* as much as their dad did, but they usually ate a lot of *chin-chin*. They each took three pieces when the plate was passed around.

"I'm not stupid, mister. This isn't a farm, it's an alley. Don't forget my cocktail, Keisha."

"How can you keep alligators in an alley?" Zeke asked, spreading a napkin on his lap.

Grandma sighed and sipped her milk. "Where's the parasol? Just because it's milk, I don't get a parasol?" Keisha found the breakfast parasol on the counter and hoped Grandma wouldn't notice the pomegranate stains on the stem. She slipped it in the milk while Grandma scanned the papers she'd printed.

"It's all right here in black and white," Grandma said, tossing the papers to the center of the table and taking off her glasses.

Mama looked around, checking for missing diners. "Razi, stop that clicking and come out from under the table."

Every once in a while, when Razi got busy with his locks and keys, the rest of the family forgot about him. Daddy lifted Razi up, carried him to the sink and put his hands under the faucet.

Zeke and Zack studied the pages Grandma had printed off the computer.

"Right here . . ." Grandma leaned over, squinting. "Where are my bifocals?"

"Are they under your napkin? On the shelf in the pantry?" Keisha was the best finder of Grandma's glasses.

"No, no." Grandma got very cross when she couldn't find her glasses. She refused to put them on a chain around her neck because that was one of the top ten indicators of looking old, according to her TV show.

Mama ignored the interruptions and said grace. When she was finished, she looked at Keisha. "Pass the greens before they get cold."

"In your pocket? Check your sweater pocket."

"I just put mine right in the *egusi* and they stay warm," Mr. Sanders said.

Grandma looked at Mr. Sanders. "You're crazy, mister."

Keisha leaned over and pulled Grandma's glasses out of her cardigan. "Please read to me about the alligator alley," she said, handing the glasses to her.

Grandma took another swig of milk and put the glasses on her nose. "I'll cut to the chase. It says here that alligators who are found in unnatural areas in Florida and who are more than four feet long and too used to humans have to be killed. But these crazy people go across state lines and take them in. I think we should mail our little bugger to Alabama."

"You can't mail an alligator!" Razi said. "The stamps won't stick."

Daddy blew on his soup. "They do have a big problem down there. It's true that when alligators and people get used to each other, it can be dangerous for both sides. Especially if humans feed alligators."

"But we feed Petunia," Razi said. "We feed her frogsicles."

"We're caring for her, Razi," Daddy said. "That's different."

"It's not nature's way for alligators and people to live close together, Razi," Mama said. "This also happened in Nigeria. When alligators try to get close for food, they can bite or kill people and then people kill them. Everyone needs to find their own food. Yours is right in front of you. Now eat."

"Which brings me to my point." Grandma had taken off her glasses again and put them on her lap. Keisha would remember that. "It's too cold here in Michigan. We can't release the reptile, so let's ship her down south."

"I'm not sure you can mail live things," Mama said. "Is that so, Mr. Sanders?"

"Well, yes and no. No to the alligators, surely. No lizards, snakes or other reptiles, either."

"Can you mail a cat?" Razi asked, tearing up his *chin-chin* and rolling it into little balls that he popped in his mouth.

"Nope. No cats, no dogs."

"Well, what can you mail, Dad?" Zack was like Grandma. He liked to get straight to the point.

"Chicks." Mr. Sanders wiped his mouth with his napkin and sat back, thinking. "Some other birds, too, I believe. I'd have to put a call in to Special Handling Services."

"What about crickets?" Razi asked.

"Jiminy Choo! How'd we get to crickets?" Grandma asked. "Let's stick with reptiles."

But Mr. Sanders was on his favorite topic, the rules and regulations of the United States Postal Service. "Crickets, yes, but not ladybugs. Bees, yes, but if I recall . . . hmmmm . . . only the queen bees. No worker bees."

"The worker bees have to take the bus!" Razi declared, as if it made perfect sense. Then, after maybe two seconds of silent bouncy-brain thinking, he added, "They have very small bus passes."

"Razi, my little one." Mama *tsk-tsk*ed. "You don't

grow big like an iroko tree by dreaming about bees and bus passes. You grow up by eating the good food that is in front of you."

It was a well-known fact that Mama did not like the size of Razi's appetite.

"You could always give it to me, Razi," Mr. Sanders said. He started to pull Razi's plate toward him. Mr. Sanders was trying that old trick of making the food seem better if Razi thought it would disappear. But Razi was thinking of bees and bus passes.

"Maybe they'll come and get her," Zeke said. "If they don't mind driving across state lines."

"Mmmmm." Mama pulled the papers over to her side of the table and looked them over. "I think Michigan may be a little far, even for alligator lovers." Mama dipped a small piece of *chin-chin* into her soup and gave it to the baby. *Chin-chin* was one of Paulo's favorites. It was very good for teething.

"With gas prices spiking all over the place, they're not coming here." Grandma put her napkin next to her bowl of *egusi*, perched her glasses on her nose, and heaved herself into a standing position. "I'm done. I need to do more research. I'll be back for dessert."

"*Chin-chin* is dessert tonight, Grandma."

"Well, then, I'll be back tomorrow for dessert."

After dinner, Keisha helped with the dishes and took the dishpan of water to the backyard to empty it on the vegetable garden. Daddy said Pumpkin-Petunia needed time alone, and even though Keisha offered, he said he should be the one to check on the alligator before bed. So Keisha went up the back stairs to the screened-in porch that jutted out from the second floor. It contained two rockers and a glider.

She knew the whole family would end up here before the end of the evening, but Keisha wanted a little time alone to watch the fireflies begin to twinkle in the dusky light.

Keisha lay on her back on the glider and put her toes on the metal armrest, rocking back and forth, back and forth, her head turned toward the darkening sky.

There were some hard things about being a wildlife rehabilitator. Not getting attached to your patients was one of them. Keisha wanted to find Pumpkin-Petunia a home, and in her secret thoughts, she even hoped to find a way for the alligator to stay with her. Alligators couldn't live in temperatures that were less than fifty degrees, so even if Carters' Urban Rescue had the right license, they would have to make room for Pumpkin-Petunia in the house. And if Mama wasn't going to make room for a puppy in the house, surely she would not make room for an alligator. And even if Mama *did* make room for an alligator, where would it live? And what kind of life could it have?

No, the only place you could imagine an alligator in Michigan was in a zoo. And Keisha understood why the zoo didn't want to take their lost alligator. They had rules at Carters' Urban Rescue, too. They only took in animals that could be rehabilitated and released back into the wild. That meant no dogs or cats or caged bunnies or hamsters or a lot of other things people brought to their door.

Back and forth, back and forth, on the glider. Keisha yawned. The door slammed downstairs and Keisha heard Razi squealing. It was time to run around in the backyard and catch fireflies in a jar. He could watch them glow for five minutes by the kitchen timer, and then he had to let them all go. Soon Daddy and Mama would be coming upstairs with their evening tea. Keisha listened. Grandma was coming, too. She scooted over to one of the rockers. Grandma pushed the glider so fast it made Keisha seasick.

"We thought we might find you up here," Daddy said, pushing the door open with his elbow. He had three cups of tea on a tray.

Grandma settled into the glider and pushed so hard she made the screens rattle.

"Did you find any more research?" Keisha asked Grandma.

Grandma pushed the glider, thinking. "How many frequent-flier miles do I have?" she asked. A few years ago, she had traveled with a group of seniors to Las Vegas. "Can I transfer those to the alligator?"

"Hmmmm . . . ," Daddy said.

"No, Grandma, my lovely," Mama said. "No alligators on the plane."

"In the cargo hold. I'm not senile," Grandma said. "I was just wondering if they'd be willing to deal."

"Scooch over, Mom." Daddy settled in next to Grandma. "I asked Dan that the other day," he said, handing Grandma her tea. "There are very strict rules regarding transporting live cargo. Few airlines will do it anymore, and unless you are a recognized dealer, all the packages have to be taken apart and searched. That would be very expensive and very stressful for our alligator friend."

"How expensive?" Grandma asked.

"Well, it costs more than three hundred dollars to transport a frog."

"Goodness gracious, what is the world coming to?" Mama asked. "When people are going hungry. We have frogs with airline tickets now."

"Well, I'm still waiting on the alligator sanctuary that just opened up in Michigan," Grandma said. "He's got a waiting list for the full-sized ones, so I took a picture of ours on my cell phone and sent it to him. I'm hoping she's small enough to get in."

"I'm sorry, Mom." Daddy lowered his teacup and turned to face his mother. "Did I miss something?"

"David Critchlow. The herpetologist. He's been rescuing them and keeping them in his basement for ten years. He finally decided to take the plunge and create a sanctuary. It opened last month."

Mama put her cup down, too. "Grandma, are you saying that there is a place for alligators here in Michigan? What about the wintertime?"

"He's working on the shelter now. It will be done by August. He's just south of Battle Creek. At last count, he had forty-two. Pumpkin-Petunia would make forty-three."

All the Carters stared at Grandma.

From down below, Razi shouted, "Look at my flashlight, everybody. It's jumping!"

"What are you people looking at?" Grandma said. "Haven't you ever heard of an alligator sanctuary before?"

Chapter Eleven

Keisha, Daddy and Grandma could not agree on who missed the sign for the highway turnoff to Interstate 94. They pulled off at Vicksburg, bumped to a stop at a roadside stand and bought two quarts of strawberries. The woman who sold them the berries pointed her finger and said, "Just take that road till you can't take it no more, turn right and look for the alligator sign."

Though Razi had begged, Mama said she could not endure her son's energy and forty-three alligators in the same field, even if there was a sturdy fence. She consoled Razi by agreeing to go with Mr. and Mrs. Sanders, the twins and a very large beach umbrella to Millennium Park, where Razi could chase the seagulls to his heart's content and Mama didn't have to worry about his losing any limbs.

"Look, Daddy, the sign says Athens . . . right!"

Mr. Carter swung the truck to the right, and Keisha and Grandma each took a side of the road to watch.

"Cow . . . cow . . . barn . . . ," Grandma reported.

"Farm . . . farm . . . barn . . . field . . . ," Keisha answered back. "Look!"

A big hand-painted sign read LIVE ALLIGATORS ON DISPLAY!

Daddy turned in and parked his truck in the shade of a huge semi from Wisconsin, with a sign on the side that read SUPPLYING CHEESE CURDS TO THE NATION.

The sun was so high overhead that they almost didn't have shadows. Keisha put her hands up to shade her eyes. Grandma began rummaging through her bag for some sort of sun protection. She found nothing.

Grandma looked up at the sky as if it had done something wrong. "I thought we'd be indoors," she said. "Hmmmm . . . maybe in the gift shop." Grandma took Keisha's arm and began dragging her in the direction of a long, low building.

She yanked open the screen door and a little string of bells flew toward them, just missing Grandma's head. Inside, it was dark and cool, and that made Grandma calm down a little. She kept moving in a straight line toward a bank of aquariums filled with turtles and snakes.

"Would you like to feed our bearded dragon from Australia?"

Keisha was almost as tall as the lady who spoke, and because of that, she found herself face to face with a very large white lizard. The lizard clung to the lady's shirt. She held out a palmful of dandelion heads.

"I'm Carmen Critchlow," she said. "Welcome to our reptile display and gift shop."

"That's no alligator," Grandma said, squinting in the low light.

Carmen laughed. "No, no. He's a lizard . . . from Australia. Alligators aren't the only reptiles that people no longer want around."

Carmen had a deep voice and sparkly dark eyes. Keisha took a dandelion head, put it on her flat palm and held out her hand so that the lizard could see it. She watched his eye rotate in the direction of the fuzzy yellow flower, and then, in an instant, his neck grew long and twisted so that his head was over the flower. Keisha felt a slight pressure and the flower head was gone.

"Impressive." Grandma leaned in for a better look. "We could use him in our front yard."

"Yes." Carmen laughed again and stroked the back of the white lizard. "Everyone says that. We should rent him out."

Carmen returned the bearded dragon to his tank. "Have you been out to see the alligators yet?"

"My grandma wanted to ask about sunblock. My dad's out back. We brought you another alligator."

"You must be Keisha!"

"And I'm Alice," Grandma said, pumping Carmen's

hand. "We spoke on the phone. I don't see any sun-block around here."

"We don't sell it, but I had some here somewhere. There's not much left. . . ." Carmen reached beneath the counter and pulled out a wrinkled tube.

"That's okay," Keisha said. "I can squeeze out enough."

"I'll have Daddy put it on," she told Grandma, taking a few steps toward the door. "Thank you, Carmen."

"I can't be out in that sun without protection. Maybe while you're out there boiling, I'll look for a lit-tle something for Razi," Grandma said. "Did we bring the credit card?"

Keisha wasn't sure, but she didn't want to say no. How wonderful if Grandma would forget about her and shop! She stepped outside and ran toward the fenced-in area behind the gift shop. This was where the alligators would be.

Their enclosure was in a big flat place with woods on one side and a cornfield on the other. At the far end of the enclosure was a tall fence. Keisha saw Daddy backing up his truck. It disappeared behind the tall fence. That must be the place where Pumpkin-Petunia was being taken.

A row of children and a few adults stood in another area looking over a three-foot fence. The fence poles were strong two-by-fours crossed with wire. As Keisha got closer, she could see there were two fences, about three feet apart. That meant children couldn't put their arms through the fence and reach the alligators.

A tall, tanned man holding a broom handle came out from behind the fence and approached the crowd that had gathered. Keisha wondered if he was David Critchlow. To get to the front of the pen, he had to walk around a pond about half the size of the city pool. The pond was lined with some kind of black fabric that was held down every few feet with used tires.

That's when Keisha saw the alligators. Dozens of pairs of eyes and nostrils were bobbing in the water. With all her alligator knowledge, Keisha had never seen alligators do this. They seemed happy to her, floaty, like clouds.

Instead of coming to the front of the enclosure, the man walked slowly around the edge of the pond, stepping over alligators and examining big-leaved plants lined up in black pots, which Keisha thought he must be ready to plant in the ground soon. As he moved a coil of hose, one of the larger alligators in the pond suddenly raised its head high in the air and brought it down—*smack!*—on the surface of the water.

"What was *that*?" asked a boy in a blue baseball cap. His mama pulled him toward her as if the alligator were about to launch itself over the fence.

"Mister, will you give it another piece of charcoal?" A little girl in a playsuit, even younger than Razi, was pointing at the alligators. She looked afraid and fascinated at the same time.

The man laughed. "All in good time. And it's

David, by the way. I like that a lot better than 'mister.' We're just getting a new recruit in the back, and I wanted to make sure we had the pen ready.

"That head slap you saw just now was one of seven vocalizations we know that alligators make. As far as I can tell, that one is closest to a teenager's whoop and holler."

As David took up his position by the fence opposite the crowd of onlookers, Keisha watched the alligators in the water and all around him. They seemed to move a little closer to him. . . . It was as if they hadn't noticed him before and now they started to pay attention.

"You see, every time I come into the enclosure, I need the alligators to see me doing other things. It wouldn't be very good for them *or* for me if they just associated me with food."

"Put another rock on his tongue. Pleeeease!"

Daddy came up behind Keisha and grabbed her shoulders. "Mission accomplished," he whispered in her ear.

"Can I see her before we leave?" Keisha whispered back.

Daddy glanced up at David. "I think so," he said.

"All right, all right," David said. He held up something in his hand. It did look like a piece of brown charcoal.

"Not many people know that Purina Mills makes a food that is the perfect blend of vitamins, minerals and fiber for alligators. This is pretty much what we feed our group here. Unless they do something *really* big in training. Then they get a frozen rat or a quail."

"I didn't know you could train alligators," an older lady in a very OL pair of elastic-waist pants said.

"Oh, you can train alligators. You just have to know what their limits are."

While David was speaking, Keisha noticed a medium-sized alligator stepping slowly toward him. At first, it put its head on one of David's big wader boots. Then it curled its body in a half circle just behind David. Was this David's special alligator? Keisha wondered. The one that was most like his pet?

"Are you training them for the circus?" the little boy wanted to know.

"No, no, nothing like that." Though the alligator was behind him, David seemed to know it was there, because when it opened its mouth and let out a hiss, David turned and poked the back of its neck with the broom handle.

Before anyone could stop him, the boy put his feet in the rungs of the first fence and began to climb. "Why are you hitting him? Don't do that."

In one quick move, Daddy lifted the boy off the fence and set him next to his mother. David tipped his hat in appreciation.

"I'm not hitting him. I'm correcting him. That's a sensitive area, and they don't like that, just as I don't like to be hissed at."

Alligators were very cute, but Keisha thought she might not like having a congregation of them all around her. Right now, David had at least two dozen behind him. Most were in the pond, a few were in muddy wallows around the pond's edge and more were using that slow half crawl that brought them closer and closer until they settled around his feet.

"But they like you," the little girl said. "Look, they're all coming closer."

"Correction. They like this." David held up the piece of alligator food.

Twisting his cap backward, the little boy kicked at the fence. "What do you train them for, then?"

"Well, as they get bigger, we want to be able to move them." David pointed to the other side of the field. "In August, we'll be putting them in their winter enclosure at night. It's hard to make an alligator move if he doesn't want to."

"So you can say 'come,' just like I do to my dog?"

"Well, it's a bit more complicated than training a dog because alligators don't respond to language as well as dogs do. But with some hard work, S-P-O-T here"— David used his broom handle to point to an alligator standing off to the side—"has been trained to come forward for his treat."

Keisha glanced around at the little crowd that had grown to five, maybe six children her brother's age. No one yelled out the name Spot as Razi would have done.

Suddenly Grandma was behind her, rustling a big paper bag. Keisha had been thinking about using her allowance to buy Razi a plastic poison dart frog, but it looked like maybe Grandma had it covered.

"Spot, come," David said. Nothing happened.

David leaned over so that he was closer to the alligator that must be Spot. How could he tell them apart? "Spot, come!"

Suddenly Spot lifted his body off the ground. With four or five quick steps, he was at David's feet. He opened his mouth.

David tossed the alligator chow into the back of his mouth. At the moment Spot's piece of alligator chow disappeared, three other alligators opened their mouths and hissed.

"Watch out!" Grandma squeezed Keisha's shoulder hard. "You're about to be gator chow, David!"

David straightened. "They're like little kids pounding on the table. They want me to know they're ready, too."

"Well, in my neighborhood, that's a fighting noise."

"You can't judge alligators by the way you think," David told Grandma. "These guys"—he circled his broom handle all around him—"they're just frogs with teeth."

Big teeth, Keisha thought. Lots and lots of them.

A tractor sputtered by on the road, and a couple of the bigger "frogs with teeth" arched their necks so that their heads were up out of the water. Then they commenced to bellow. It was such a powerful noise, in addition to the tractor, which was doing a pretty good job making a powerful noise itself, that the children looked uncertain. Some covered their ears.

"This is worse than the motocross," said the boy in the blue baseball cap, pressing his hands to his ears.

David shouted over the noise, "It's just instinctive. They are responding to the noise as if there are other alligators in the area. They do that sometimes with tractors, motorcycles. . . . You should hear what they do when it thunders."

The children didn't look too happy about this possibility.

"Okay, so should we get a big one out here? Look out at the pond. You see lots of heads over there. Which one is the biggest?"

David waited as the children jostled and pointed. It was generally agreed that the alligator in the center of the pond, the one that floated with most of its back showing as well as its eyes and nose, was the biggest.

"You're right! Claudius is our biggest alligator, but he used to be much bigger. He came from a zoo where he was in a very small pen. No one exercised him. They just fed him. He was four hundred pounds. He was so fat he couldn't walk. He just scooted over the ground. We had to put him on a diet. Any guesses on what is alligator diet food?"

Suggestions bubbled up from the group around the enclosure. "Lettuce? Birdseed?"

David formed a zero with his fingers. "Nothing. No food for nine months. As you might imagine, he didn't like us very much. We made him waddle around for some exercise, but no food. He's much better now. A trim three hundred pounds. So get your cameras ready. I'm going to call Claudius."

David waited while people dug in their bags.

"Claudius. Come!"

Unlike Spot, Claudius did not need a repeat invitation. Water streamed away from his snout as he lifted himself out of the water and his legs paddled him forward. There were a few alligators between Claudius and the food in David's hand. Claudius churned over them, stepping on heads and backs. The alligators near David scuttled away. Claudius was the king. He was the size of a movie alligator! Keisha thought he must be at least twelve feet long. When he opened his mouth, David dropped two pellets in. With one swallow, they were gone.

Claudius liked his food! The cameras clicked away.

Keisha heard her name being called. She turned to see Carmen hurrying toward them with a squirming bundle in her arms.

"I thought before you left, you would like to hold our little guy, Alphabet Soup."

The other children crowded around Carmen and Keisha.

"Let me see! Can I hold him, too?"

The alligator lay still in Carmen's hands, his little legs dangling, as if being carried by a human being was almost too much for him to handle. He was not even half the size of Pumpkin-Petunia and had a band around his mouth.

"Why isn't he with the other ones?" the girl in the playsuit wanted to know.

"Because he's too small yet," Carmen told her. "They might eat him. Or a blue heron or a sandhill crane might make him into dinner."

"Lady, can I hold that, too?" asked the boy in the baseball cap.

"I'm going to show Keisha how to hold him first. You have to hold him in a special way to keep control," Carmen said.

She took Keisha's right hand and placed her palm just beneath the alligator's front legs. "Now curl your index finger up around its neck and close your left hand around its back legs." As soon as Carmen had transferred Alphabet Soup to Keisha, the little alligator started twisting all over the place.

"Just hold on," Carmen said. "He's doing the death roll."

Keisha was too polite to tell Carmen that she knew what the death roll was. She tried not to fight the alligator but to hold on and let him wriggle.

"Keisha." Daddy had come up behind her. He was letting her know that he was there if she needed him.

"This is what the alligator was doing with Dan, re-member?"

"The death roll?" Keisha asked, taking some deep breaths.

Just as suddenly as it had begun twisting and turn-ing, the alligator stopped. It lay limp in Keisha's hands, its little legs dangling again, eyes closed. Keisha held him up so that she could see his second eyelid, the scales behind his ear holes, his needle-like teeth. She didn't

care what anybody said about alligators. She thought they were adorable.

"You can see why kids would want one," Carmen said to the crowd around them. "What I tell children when they ask their parents to buy them an alligator is: What would happen if I put *you* in a little tank? You'd still grow big, wouldn't you?"

"Sweetie . . ." Daddy took Keisha's hand. "We better collect Grandma and say good-bye."

Keisha asked Daddy if she could sit on his shoulders. She wanted to see the alligator sanctuary from a bird's-eye view. Daddy understood. He bent down and Keisha got on. She looked at the alligators rolling in the grass. She watched them lying in their wallows and floating on the edge of the pond as if suspended. Every rescued alligator deserved a place like this.

Keisha leaned over to whisper in Daddy's ear, "Can we visit Pumpkin-Petunia now?"

Daddy looked over at David, who was talking to a new group of visitors. He pointed to the back enclosure, the one behind the big fence. David gave him a thumbs-up. Daddy started off at a trot that joggled Keisha so much she had to grab his head.

"My eyes! I'm blind." He turned around in a circle.

"Daddy!" Keisha giggled. "People are looking."

"Oh, in that case." Daddy went down on one knee so Keisha could climb off. "We don't want anyone following us." They walked around the corner of the enclosure. Several big pens had been set up, with high walls around the sides and back and the same wire fencing at the front. There were much larger alligators in the first and second pens. The third seemed to be empty, except for a little rustling grass near the back of the pen, where the uncut grass grew tall. That was where Keisha thought Pumpkin-Petunia might be hiding. She looked around the big pen and noticed it had its very own wallow.

"Can I take a picture of Pumpkin-Petunia and her wallow?" she asked. "To show Razi?"

"Sure." Daddy handed Keisha his cell phone.

Keisha stood quietly, waiting for a glimpse of Pumpkin-Petunia, but her scaly friend didn't want to be around humans at the moment. Keisha thought maybe she'd had enough of humans for a while. Though it was hard to say good-bye, Keisha felt so much better about her little alligator's life now. Pumpkin-Petunia could be around other alligators—when she grew big enough, so they wouldn't eat her. She would be in a large pen with grass and muddy places just like her native home.

It wasn't a perfect happy-movie ending for Pumpkin-Petunia because she could never go back to the wild. But when Razi told the story, Pumpkin-Petunia would "and then" herself to a pretty good "the end" here at the Critchlow Alligator Sanctuary. And Keisha would even be able to visit her!

She settled for taking pictures of the big alligators and the wallows. As she was reviewing the pictures of the big muddy holes, she said, "Maybe I won't show these to Razi. Maybe we'll just keep these for reference."

"Good point," Daddy said. "Why give Razi more ideas than he already has?"

Chapter Twelve

Back home, Keisha watched Razi splashing in the bath-tub and thought about what Carmen had said about alligators and how they didn't stop growing big.

"Razi, did you know that a baby alligator will grow about a foot a year? Boy alligators grow up to fifteen feet, and girl alligators are around nine."

"That's past my eyebrows," Razi said, sticking a clump of bubble-bath foam on his chin. "I want to get out now. Close your eyes, Keisha."

Keisha closed her eyes. She was wondering how she could teach people that those cute little alligator hatchlings could grow big. She grabbed the bath towel and held it out to Razi, closing her eyes until she heard the water slosh.

"Razi, don't forget to shake off before you step—"

Too late. Razi was climbing over the side of the tub. Keisha pressed her eyes closed again. Water flew everywhere. Razi must be dancing from foot to foot.

"Just put something on so I can see again!"

"It's time to measure me. You can open your eyes."

Dressed in his pajama bottoms, Razi had pulled the towel around him like a superhero cape.

Keisha rub-a-dubbed Razi with the towel until Mama appeared in the bathroom doorway.

"Do you think you grow like a reed, Mr. Razi Carter? I just measured you a few days ago."

"I grow like an alligator!" Razi said. "A foot a year."

There was a place behind the bathroom door where the Carters kept a pencil record of the children as they grew. Mama had put a small mark in red for every foot so the children could see their progress. Razi stood there, his damp head making a spot on the wall.

The image of Razi waiting to be measured inspired Keisha. "Razi, that's a great idea!"

Keisha handed Mama Razi's towel and ran to find the phone. When Aaliyah picked up, Keisha could barely contain her excitement: "I think I know how we can make some money for the alligator sanctuary *and* educate people about not buying alligator babies *and* get some free advertising for Carters' Urban Rescue," she said, all in one breath. "I just don't know how we're going to market it."

"Let me get my lemonade," Aaliyah said, "and a piece of paper."

* * *

The next morning, Daddy took Razi and the baby to the park because Keisha needed kids who colored inside the lines. Zeke and Zack and Aaliyah and Wen all volunteered. Grandma Alice found a copyright-free drawing of an alligator on the Internet, and Mama projected it on the wall. The children copied it onto a piece of butcher paper, which they then spread out on the kitchen table to make the Alligator Growth Chart, brought to you by Carters' Urban Rescue.

Everyone began to color in the alligator. Grandma had to raid her own colored-pencil box to get enough greens.

From her research on the Internet, Aaliyah thought the poster should be three feet long and would hang between three and six feet from the floor. It's at those heights that most kids want to know how fast they're growing. This meant that the children only had room to picture the alligator from tummy to snout, but Mama said that was okay because children could imagine the rest.

"Perfect," Mama said. "When they grow close to the top, they will be teenagers, and yet this is the size of a six-year-old alligator."

"How are we going to copy this?" Aaliyah asked. "Do we have a budget? Color copies cost a lot of money."

"Mr. Malone told Daddy he would help us out using the zoo's big printer in the education office."

Zeke stood back, examining their efforts. "Hmmm . . . it still needs something. How about if we say here: 'You're as high as an alligator eye'?"

"Good idea, but you have to print neat."

"Let Wen do it. She's got the best handwriting."

They worked all morning, with only one *chin-chin* and pomegranate juice break.

It looked so real. Wen had even drawn in the scales.

Admiring their artwork, Keisha said, "Now maybe people will think about it. Alligators get big just like little boys do."

"And girls," Aaliyah reminded Keisha.

"I'm so proud of all of you," Mama said, brushing away the eraser crumbs. "Little by little, the bird builds its nest. Now maybe we have helped the poor alligators by showing others what a big job caring for a baby alligator can become."

"It's almost finished . . ." Keisha wasn't sure what, but there was still something missing. She knew it was true that these big alligators were once so small, but it was hard to imagine that even Pumpkin-Petunia could have fit between the ends of a ruler as a baby.

"This alligator looks big, like the alligators you see in the zoo. But how would you know the cute little baby gator you're thinking about buying is going to grow big like this?"

Daddy and Razi and the baby arrived home from the park, just as they were putting the finishing touches on the poster.

As soon as Razi saw them in the kitchen, he said, "Look what I got, everybody." He was holding up one of the little airplanes they sold by the lemonade stands for a quarter. Razi launched his plane and it landed—

ping!—on the kitchen table. Everyone looked up at once, shifting the drawing.

"Razi!" the children cried out in unison. Razi stuck out his lip.

"I miss Pumpkin-Petunia," he said. "I want an alligator to play with."

"Oh, for heaven's sake, Razi." Grandma had been trying to draw an alligator toenail. When the paper moved, her pencil slipped. "We don't have enough bathtubs!"

"Just a baby, then. I'll keep him in the sink."

Keisha looked at the plane lying near the bottom of the poster. "You've done it again, Razi! That's what this poster needs—a drawing of a little alligator at the bottom so people can see the difference. Most people have seen a grown-up alligator at the zoo or on TV, but not a baby one. And maybe, maybe—"

"We could put a couple other ideas of things they could buy from the Reptile Shack that wouldn't get big," Wen said. She must have been excited because Wen never interrupted.

"Yes, that's perfect!" Keisha said. It helped to give positive choices. "A little gecko or a salamander would be a better pet."

"I want a gecko or a salamander!" Razi said. "Please, Mama!"

"You know we don't own pets, little one. We have animals out back right now. Go visit them."

"But I want one that stays."

This conversation had been going on for so long that everyone knew what Mama would say ("Then you better find us another profession") and then what Razi would say ("I would keep it in my bedroom and you wouldn't even see it") and then what Grandma would say ("That's a serving of wind pudding with a topping of air sauce").

Every once in a while, Keisha would question Mama's rule, testing what it would really mean to have an animal stay instead of go. She knew it wasn't very practical to have an alligator as a pet, but some people did it. And now that she had experience . . .

Aaliyah was writing furiously on her tablet.

"But where can we sell the posters?" Zack asked.

"Maybe door to door like with World's Finest Chocolate?" Zeke suggested. Their 4-H Wild 4-Ever Club had done a fund-raiser like that last year.

Aaliyah kept writing with her left hand and put her finger up with her right. This meant she was about to say something market-savvy.

Zeke sighed. Sometimes it took a while for Aaliyah's bright ideas to emerge, and everyone was supposed to stay quiet until she finished.

This time, however, it didn't take long. "Well, since Wen suggested the Reptile Shack, maybe they would sell them there. But I was also thinking . . . the Hollyhock Parade. We could sell them at the picnic."

Keisha moved closer to see what Aaliyah was drawing. Every year on the Fourth of July, hundreds of neighbors gathered to celebrate and cheer for the local children on their decorated bicycles.

Aaliyah held up her picture. "We can decorate the Red Rider Wagon like an alligator float."

"Wait a minute," Zack said. "How does making your wagon look like an alligator sell posters?"

But Keisha followed Aaliyah's thinking. Sometimes she could picture things in her mind, and then all she had to do was work backward, step by step, to make them happen. The Hollyhock Parade was perfect. Kids sold all sorts of stuff at the picnic afterward—the toys they didn't want or the bead jewelry they made, and once Razi even sold rocks he'd found by the side of the road. Razi was a good salesman.

"We can do it at the kids' bazaar afterward," Keisha said. "Razi can be our salesperson."

"Are we going to sell alligators, too?" Razi asked. "The baby ones? Can I have one?"

Keisha, Aaliyah and Wen gave each other the LBL

(Little-Brother Look), which was when you made your eyes very wide and then rolled them. Aaliyah was an only child, but Wen had a baby brother, too, between Paulo's and Razi's ages. Keisha kept telling her, "Just wait."

But right after the LBL, Keisha snuck a look at Mama. Maybe, just maybe, if they rescued another alligator as a baby, Keisha could take care of it until it was so big it needed to go to the alligator sanctuary. That would take a couple of years.

But Mama was all about business. "I saw a pattern for an alligator costume. If I sew a big one, Razi can use it for Halloween."

"I want alligator swimming goggles." Razi jumped up and down. "Standard-issue!"

"Let me see that drawing, Aaliyah," Mama said. "I'll put it on the refrigerator and give this idea time to grow."

"Well, it better not grow in alligator time." Grandma got up from her chair. "We only have a few weeks. Besides, I have to get to my yoga class."

Grandma liked to learn something new every year. This year, she'd spotted an ad in *On-the-Town* magazine for a class called Yoga You Can Do.

Mama sat down next to Aaliyah.

Keisha took Grandma's chair and studied the poster.

She put her hand over Mama's. "You never know. There might be a baby alligator out there right now who needs us to help it find a home before winter."

How do you keep track of the days during summer vacation? After seventeen visits to the public pool, six visits to the library, twenty games of hip-hopscotch and four bicycle rides to Millennium Park to get rainbow sherbet push-ups, it was Fourth of July and time for Alger Heights' annual Hollyhock Parade.

It didn't happen exactly the way Keisha had pictured it in her mind.

No. It was even better.

Mama sewed alligator costumes for Razi and baby Paulo. Paulo sat in the wagon, and Razi ran alongside making alligator vocalizations. He carried a poster-board sign taped on a stick that said I'M A FIVE-YEAR-OLD ALLIGATOR.

Daddy ran behind Razi holding his tail so it wouldn't trip him. When that didn't work, he gave the sign to Keisha and picked Razi up so

he could wave his arms and legs like an alligator. Keisha was embarrassed because she was clearly bigger than a five-year-old alligator, but she held the sign up high so people would get the idea.

Zeke and Zack stayed on either side of the wagon in case Paulo decided to climb out, and Keisha pulled it. People laughed and called Daddy the human float.

Even though he had to put an ice pack on his lower back for the rest of the day, he said it was worth it because Carters' Urban Rescue got $127 in donations for the alligator sanctuary at the picnic.

But the best part came after Keisha overheard an argument between Razi and his classmate Marco Brown. She was sitting on the swings, sipping the last little bit of her lemon ice, when Marco rushed by with the alligator head of Razi's costume.

"Give it," Razi was calling after him. "I'm telling my daddy."

Mama, who'd just finished a sale of four posters to Ms. Tellerico, the principal at their school, reached out and grabbed Razi by the collar.

Marco stopped running, too, and said, "So? My daddy is bigger than your daddy."

"Is not. My daddy is bigger than your daddy." Razi buried his head in Mama's dress.

Marco was running back to Razi, but then he saw Mama and stopped quick.

"My daddy is bigger than a full-sized alligator!" Razi shouted, holding Mama tight.

"Boys! That's not how we talk," Ms. Tellerico said in her principal voice. "Use your words in a nice way and save all that alligator knowledge for science lab." Ms. Tellerico held out her hand for the alligator head, which Marco handed over.

"Now come over here and meet my nephew. Jack, this is Marco and Razi."

Jack was holding on to a leash that ended somewhere under the sale table. Out rolled a fluffy puppy at the end of the leash.

"A puppy!" Razi said. "Mama, I want a puppy!" Razi bent down, and the puppy jumped up and gave him puppy kisses. Razi was a messy eater. The puppy had a lot to lick.

Marco sat down cross-legged. He knew what he had to do to get a turn with the puppy. Daddy came around from the sale table and sat next to Marco.

Puppies could do that, Keisha thought as she watched Razi go from near tears to giggling as he held the puppy.

"Can I have a turn?" Marco asked.

Jack leaned down and took the wiggling bundle in his hands. "You have to hold it like this," he said, showing the kids how to support the puppy's legs. Keisha had already learned that with Alphabet Soup, but she didn't say so.

"Can we have a puppy, Mama? Please?" Razi begged. "I'll keep it in my bedroom. You won't even have to see it!"

"Puppies don't belong in the bedroom. They need to be watched," Mama said sternly.

"My sister has a crate in the kitchen," Ms. Tellerico said. "That's where Penny sleeps."

"Yes," Mama agreed. She put her hand on Daddy's shoulder, and he looked up at her. "Puppies have to sleep in a crate."

Oooh, this was something Keisha would have to remember. Mama didn't say yes, but Mama didn't say no, either.

And when Mama didn't say no, that left a tiny little space for a possibility to grow. Maybe not for a baby alligator. That possibility was too big for the space between Mama's yes and Mama's no.

But maybe for something furry and fluffy, something small and . . . puppy?

Alligator Fact File

- Alligators belong to a family of reptiles called crocodilians. Crocodiles and alligators are very similar, and are the last living reptiles dating back to the dinosaurs. The easiest way to tell the difference between the two is that alligators have a wider snout that packs more crushing power for small prey like turtles, while crocodiles have a narrower, longer snout that is better for catching fish and mammals.

- About one foot long at birth, alligators grow a foot or so every year until they reach adulthood at about seven years of age if they are given proper nutrition.

- Female alligators grow to be 6 to 9 feet in length, while male alligators reach 12 to 15 feet when they are full-grown (the longest measured alligator was over 19 feet!). They live to be about 30 years old in the wild and up to 50 years, or longer in rare cases, in captivity.

- Most alligators in captivity are smaller than normal because they don't live in proper-sized cages and aren't fed a complete diet.

- Experts estimate that there are several thousand captive alligators living in northern states. The hatchlings are easy to find locally or, if that's illegal, on the Internet.

- If you Google "Gator on the Loose," you'll see plenty of news stories and videos from around the country about escaped pet alligators.

WHATEVER THE DILEMMA, IF IT'S GOT FUR OR FEATHERS (OR SCALES!) THE CARTERS ARE THE ONES TO CALL!

Dear Readers,

I got the idea for an alligator in the city pool because we really did have a three-foot alligator running around one of our southeast-side neighborhoods on Labor Day weekend in 2007. A courageous young woman coaxed it into a cat carrier with a broom. As you know from reading the story, zoos are not set up to take in orphaned animals but to help out in a pinch. Dan Malone, the animal management supervisor at John Ball Zoo here in Grand Rapids, offered to take the alligator home. During the TV coverage, however, the alligator's owner called to ask for it back. While he was moving, the alligator had escaped from a box.

My plan all along was for the children in *Gator on the Loose!* to have a bake sale to raise the money to mail the alligator to a sanctuary in the southeastern United States. But when I did my research, I found out that that wasn't realistic. If rain forest frogs cost several hundred dollars to transport, can you imagine how much a three-foot alligator would cost? That's a lot of cupcakes and brownies! What could I do?

Then I read about an alligator sanctuary right here in Michigan. It's true! The Critchlow Alligator Sanctuary is located in a former farm field in Athens, a town about an hour and a half south of my home. Owners David and Carmen Critchlow used to keep their rescued alligators in their basement. Now forty-five alligators live in the sanctuary, which operates on proceeds from ticket and gift-shop sales, as well as donations. It's a strange sight to be driving through farm country and see a sign that says, "Live Alligators on Display."

But that's why we writers say that truth can be stranger than fiction.

I was so thrilled to discover this sanctuary because now my story could have a realistic happy ending. When we visited, I "adopted" two alligators and so got to name them—Pumpkin and Petunia, of course.

Visit the Critchlow Alligator Sanctuary on the Web at www.alligatorsanctuary.com.

Happy reading!
Sue

Acknowledgments

I am especially indebted to my longtime editor, Nancy Hinkel, for asking me to propose a book idea I thought kids would enjoy. Assistant editor Allison Wortche worked closely with Nancy and me to shape the characters and plot. My agent Wendy Schmalz's support also proved indispensable. In addition to these wonderful people, a whole team of super-creative people at Random House, including the designer, Sarah Hokanson, as well as illustrator Priscilla Lamont, worked hard to create this beautiful book. Thank you!

About the Author

Sue Stauffacher lives with her husband and sons in a 150-plus-year-old farmhouse in the city of Grand Rapids, Michigan. Over the years, possums, bats, raccoons, mice, squirrels, crows, ducks, woodchucks, chipmunks, voles, skunks, bunnies, and a whole bunch of other critters have lived on the property. Though Sue is not a rehabilitator herself, she is passionate about helping kids know what to do when the wild meets the child.

Sue's novels for young readers include *Harry Sue, Donutheart,* and *Donuthead,* which *Kirkus Reviews* called "touching, funny, and gloriously human" in a starred review. Her most recent picture book, *Nothing but Trouble,* won the NAACP Image Award for Outstanding Literary Work—Children. Besides writing children's books, Sue is a frequent visitor to schools as a speaker and literacy consultant, drawing on two decades of experience as a journalist, educator, and program administrator. To learn more about Sue and her books, visit her on the Web at www.suestauffacher.com.